Definitely
DAPHNE

by Tami Charles

STONE ARCH BOOKS
a capstone imprint

_ne_ is published by Stone Arch Books
 ıprint
 st Drive
 .ato, Minnesota 56003
 pstone.com

ibrary of Congress Cataloging-in-Publication Data is available on the
Library of Congress website.

Summary: In front of her followers, Daphne is a hilarious, on-the-rise vlog
star. But at school Daphne is the ever-skeptical Annabelle Louis, seventh-
grade super geek and perennial new kid. To cope with her mom's upcoming
military assignment in Afghanistan and her start at a brand-new middle
school, Annabelle's parents send her to a therapist. Dr. Varma insists
Annabelle try stepping out of her comfort zone, hoping it will give her the
confidence to make friends, which she'll definitely need once Mom is gone.
Luckily there is one part of the assignment Annabelle DOES enjoy—her vlog,
Daphne Doesn't, in which she appears undercover and gives hilarious takes
on activities she thinks are a waste of time. She is great at entertaining her
online fans, yet her classmates don't know she exists. Can Annabelle keep up
the double life forever?

ISBN 978-1-68436-031-4 (hardcover)
ISBN 978-1-68436-032-1 (reflowable epub)

Cover illustration by Marcos Calo
Design by Kay Fraser

Printed and bound in Canada.
PA020

This book is dedicated to my bestie, my chica, my favorite "dork" of all, Stephanie Jones. I appreciate all the advice during early Daphne drafts. But truly, I'm excited to witness your own writing journey. I can't wait to see you soar!

I'd also like to dedicate this book to all of my Linden third- and fifth-grade students. Thank you for giving me the green light to follow my dreams.

To my cousin Ruben, for sharing your funny (and sometimes sad) Air Force childhood stories with me. ¡Gracias por todo!

Lastly, special thanks to my therapist-friend, Elizabeth Rossi, MDFT Clinician at Family & Children's Aid in Connecticut. You helped me bring Dr. Varma to life!

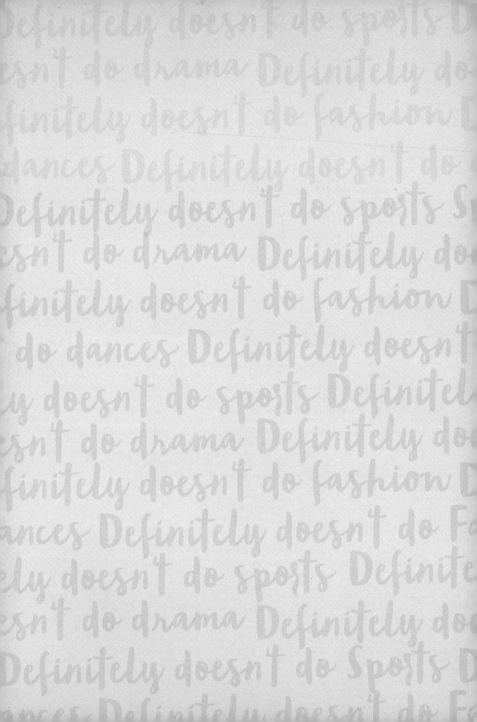

1

ALWAYS ON THE MOVE!

Confession #1: My life is one big movie series.

Confession #2: Some of the movies are "in my head." Some are as real as the ones on my MacBook computer.

I know what you're thinking: *That's crazy, girl!*

Crazy. Creative. Crafty. It's all about perspective.

Here's the latest horror film that happened yesterday in the Louis household.

Disclaimer: Some scenes may (or may not) be exaggerated for dramatic effect.

The opening credits roll in, slow and bold. . . .

Always on the Move:

The Sad, Lonely Life of an Air Force Brat

Starring: Annabelle Daphne Louis
Directed by: Annabelle Daphne Louis

It all begins on a dark and stormy Friday evening. Dad makes dinner—a fall-off-the-bone Puerto Rican stewed chicken dish called *pollo guisado*. If you have never eaten this, then you don't know what it means to feel alive.

"Family meeting in the living room!" Mom announces, just as I'm sopping up the last forkful.

Mom loves meetings. I'm more of a go-with-the-flow kind of girl. Mom holds meetings about chores, meetings about "achieving goals," and my favorite: meetings about when we're *meeting* again.

We all take a seat on the carpet, because we're not completely moved in to the new house yet. Outside, the wind is smacking a tree branch against the window. Gotta love when nature adds its own special effects. Mom lights a few candles and clicks the dimmer on the light remote. Dad clears his throat and lets out one long-winded breath. If I didn't know any better, I would think they were about to summon a ghost.

And cue camera zoom . . .

Mom starts talking. "Annabelle, we wanted to tell you the real reason we've moved to Linden. . . ."

The camera is zoomed in so close to my face, I'm sure the viewing audience can see every freckle. The skin under my eyes sinks lower and lower as seconds turn to minutes and Mom draws out her speech. The audio fades in and out, and all I hear are words like "leave" and "assignment" and "alone."

The sounds and their words mix together. I try to shake the scene out of my head. Tell myself to quit making a movie out of every moment in my life and get back to focus. But then it hits me.

"What did you say, Mom? You're getting . . . what?" My throat tightens.

TDY . . . TDY . . . TDY . . .

Temporary duty yonder. Fancy Air Force words for Mom's leaving—this time without us. The letters repeat over and over until the final image closes out.

"Wait, there's more," Mom says.

Ladies and gentlemen, we have a sequel.

Dad adds in his piece. "Since this will be Mom's last assignment before retiring next year, we're going to stay in Linden and live civilian life. She'll commute to Fort Dix for work until it's time for her TDY. And with the transfer, I landed a new Cisco client based in New York, which means I have to travel into the city a few times a week, so—"

"Slow down," I say. "What about homeschooling, Dad?"

Mom and Dad lock hands and look at each other, then back at me. I know what's coming.

I am going to middle school. Real school, with teachers and seventh graders and eyeballs and *gym*.

"You guys tricked me!" I'm standing now. The camera angles upward to make me appear larger than I am.

I should've known something was up. Just a week ago, we were living happily ever after in Germany, where Mom was Master Sergeant in the Air Force and Dad worked from home for Cisco, all while homeschooling me. Life was perfectly fine. Then Mom comes home one day and announces we're headed to the city she once lived in—Linden, New Jersey, land of Targets, Starbucks, and an oil refinery that occasionally makes the whole city smell like a gigantic fart. Her words, not mine.

She's been acting funny ever since. Extra clingy with me. Extra lovey-dovey kissy-face with Dad. UGH!

Mom and Dad spring to their feet too. The camera pans up and then zooms out.

The next scene plays out like a game of verbal Ping-Pong, with me asking questions and Mom firing back answers.

ME
How long will you be gone?

MOM
Six months, not much longer.

(A ghost whizzes by and punches ME right in the throat.)

ME
Why can't Dad and I go with you, like we always do?

MOM
I'm sorry, Annabelle. This is not like it was before in
the UK, Spain, and Germany. I cannot bring you to
Afghanistan. You understand, *schätzchen*?

*(MOM calls ME "sweetie" in German to soften the blow.
It usually works. Not this time.)*

ME
When do you leave?

MOM
After Christmas.

*(Insert massive thought bubble above my head. That's four
months from now. DAD grabs ME by the shoulders and
pulls ME in for a hug. I transform into ice, blocking out his
warmth.)*

ME
I won't go to school with a bunch of people I don't
know! It's bad enough you guys moved me away from
the one friend I have in the UK. Now you expect me to
start all over again?

(My eyes are stinging now. I will not cry. I will not cry.)

DAD
This will be a big change for everyone, Annabelle, but
together we'll get through it.

(DAD refuses to let ME go. Zoom in on MOM, wrapping her arms around us. The warmth of MOM and DAD melts my ice block, even though I don't want it to. Outside, the rain stops falling. The tree branch no longer smacks against the window. And that imaginary ghost has faded into oblivion.)

MOM
Everything will be fine, Annabelle. My Air Force buddy, Pete Fingerlin, is the counselor at McManus Middle School. I called him yesterday to explain the situation. He set you up with a buddy to give you a tour bright and early Monday morning.

ME *(thinking)*
Buddy? Sounds like a code word for babysitter. Call me psychic, but I have a feeling this whole middle school thing will go horribly wrong.

End scene!

2

TEXTING ACROSS THE POND

Mae: Belle! How's life in the US? Missing you here in the UK. :'(

Me: New country. New house. New school. New problems. Over it.

Mae: SCHOOL? Like with other humans?

Me: Apparently Mom and Dad forgot that I'm allergic to formal education.

Mae: That's awful! When do you start?

Me: T minus 4 hrs., 38 mins. Run away with me?

Mae: Oy! I forgot about the time difference. Get some sleep!

Me: About to start a new novel with Dad. "Enchanted Air." Margarita Engle strikes again! I'm missing our father-daughter homeschool sessions. . . .

Mae: You'll survive . . . maybe. ;) FaceTime ya before you leave. Sweet dreams!

3

LINDEN HATES ME

The FaceTime ringer beeps just as I'm getting ready for
jail. I mean, school. Mae Tanaka—best friend, keeper of
promises. As soon as I open the app on my iPad, I let out
a big yawn.

"You must be tired!" Mae says.

"You would be too if you'd spent the whole weekend
having nightmares."

"I still can't believe your parents sprung all of this
on you!"

When Mom was stationed in the UK, Mae was the
first friend I met on base. She and I were among the rare
kids who preferred to be homeschooled rather than go
to a new school every other year. That's the life of an
Air Force kid. Too many moves. Too many desperate
attempts to make new friends. By the time we reached
our third country, I was totally over it.

Because both of our dads were techies who worked

from home, Mae and I had the perfect setup. Our dads would take turns teaching us. My dad would take the morning shift to teach us math, technology, and sciences. And in the afternoon, Mr. Tanaka taught us how to use "nature as our classroom." We'd paint in the park, take strolls around the lake, and study foreign languages. We'd read and discuss the fine works of our favorite authors, Rita Williams-Garcia, Margarita Engle, and Kate DiCamillo.

Ah, those were the good old days.

There's a knock at my door, and I already know who it is.

"Hold on. Mom alert." I crack the door.

Mom weasels her face inside and looks at me, frowning because I'm still in my robe. "Need help getting dressed?" she asks, still wearing her *I'm-sorry* face.

"No, Mom. I'm fine. Plus, I'm FaceTiming with Mae for a couple minutes."

"Tell her hello, and don't take too long. Wouldn't want you to be late to your meeting."

Honestly, I've had enough meetings for one lifetime.

I hurry back to my iPad. It's almost seven o'clock. That doesn't give me much time, so I speed my way through everything that's happened over the weekend. Mom's TDY. The new school. The ridiculous school tour with a "buddy."

I end my rant with, "So basically my life is ruined."

Mae hits me with, "No, it isn't. You'll be amazing, Annabelle!"

Typical Mae. All rainbows and sunshine and bubbles.

I prop the iPad on my dresser. "Hold on while I get dressed," I tell her.

"Ooh, what are you going to wear?" she asks. "I can't even picture doing algebra in anything besides my pajamas."

I have yet to receive all of my boxes from Germany. In my closet, there are three boxes I still haven't unpacked. "I haven't had time to even think about that," I say, growing more frustrated as I look for clothes. Nothing seems good enough.

"You know," Mae says, "I heard Americans like color. Look for something that stands out. Ooh, like Lady Gaga!"

"I'd rather snack on broken glass."

"Just trust me!" Mae laughs.

At the bottom of one of the boxes, I find an oversized orange plaid shirt and purple leggings. I shuffle over to my dresser, still wrapped in my robe, and hold up the outfit.

"Gaga enough?" I ask.

"Oh, that's perfect!" Mae says. "Now you just need shoes."

In the closet, I find my favorite pair—teal Converse sneaker-boots. "I'm pretty sure I've forgotten how this social thing works, Mae," I say as I pull them on. "Like, who am I supposed to have lunch with? Aren't there rules and reserved tables?" I sigh really heavy as I lace them up. Then I pop my face back on the screen so Mae can see me again.

"Ta-da!" I stand back so she can get a better view of my outfit.

At first she doesn't say anything, just gives a long stare.

"Oh, no. You think I look awful, don't you?" I ask.

"Actually, no." Mae's voice gets really soft. "I think you look perfect. I just miss you is all."

I hold two fingers to my heart and wait for her to do it back. That's our thing, the number two. Because even though miles and seas and time zones separate us, we're always going to be two *amigas,* the best two mates there ever were.

There's a rapid knock on my door.

"I have to go now, Mae."

"Send me a text and let me know how it goes."

I blow her a kiss and hang up. Before I can even open my door, Mom comes in, uninvited, and plops on my bed.

"I'm sorry, Annabelle," she apologizes for the trillionth time.

And I know she means it, but it doesn't change the fact that I do not want to go to school. I do not want to just up and change everything about our family. I like the way things are. Well, *were*.

"I'll be OK, Mom," I lie, cold and quick.

"At least you have one thing to look forward to—having a separate girl cave." Mom smiles.

Usually when we moved bases, my girl cave would be in the same room as my bedroom. But with this big house, my parents promised me a room in the basement. I want to be excited, but this school thing ruined it.

"Oh, come on, Annabelle. You have to be just a little excited for your first day!"

"But it's not the first day, Mom. School started weeks ago when we were still in Germany. You do know what this means, don't you?"

"Oh, I hope you're not worried about falling behind. You are a math and technology wizard. And how many languages are you up to by now? Three?"

"Actually four." My cheeks go red. "Still, it's not about the work. It's just that by now everybody has formed their circles. That's how school works. That's why I stopped going in the first place. And now you guys are throwing me to the sharks!"

I look at myself in the mirror and contemplate doing something with my hair. In Germany, the weather was kinder to my curls. Judging by the way my hair is poofing out, Linden already hates me.

Mom lifts off the bed and stands behind me in the mirror.

"You look great, *schätzchen*. You'll amaze everyone with your charm and wit. Those kids will be begging to be your friend. I just know it!"

I'm not so sure.

4

JUST THE NEW KID

Mom and Dad insist not only on driving me to school but also on going inside to meet the counselor, Mr. Fingerlin, and my assigned "buddy."

Side note: *Is it just me, or does the name Fingerlin make you want to eat something greasy?*

We're all silent in the car. Dad turns on the radio, blasts the volume, and starts dancing. All of a sudden the rapper starts bragging about how much money he spent on clothing.

"Seventy-five hundred dollars on a coat? Man, I don't get this *new* kind of music!" Dad yells over the beat.

He and Mom start laughing. I can't help it, so I laugh too. Those lyrics *are* pretty ridiculous! Who spends that kind of money on clothes? Especially when thrift stores are the greatest creation ever? And for the first time since Mom broke the TDY news, it feels like we're back to our old selves again, the laugh-till-we-snort Louis trio.

McManus is a huge school tucked among pretty houses and tree-lined streets. Dad pulls up in front, and the red entry doors seem a thousand miles away. For the two weeks I went to school on base in the UK, it was nothing like this. Just a small group of us, spread among three or four classrooms.

Dad lowers the music, and I let out a heavy sigh.

"We'll do the tour with you, Annabelle. Help you ease in," Dad says.

"That would be super embarrassing. Please don't!"

Dad turns around to say something else, but Mom's already slamming the car door behind her and marching her heels straight up to the school.

I grab my knapsack and make a beeline toward her, stumbling over my untied Converse sneaker-boot. I could have sworn I tied it back at home. I catch myself before falling, quickly tie it again, and keep it moving.

Mr. Fingerlin and my "buddy" are opening the doors by the time I reach Mom. I'm out of breath, Dad is shuffling behind me, and Mom is giving Mr. Fingerlin a bear hug.

I have to admit, I'm kind of disappointed that Mr. Fingerlin doesn't look like Colonel "Fingerlick'n Good" Sanders. That's the mascot for Kentucky Fried Chicken. Believe it or not, we had plenty of those back in Germany.

"Aim high!" Mr. Fingerlin throws his bald head back and points his face to the sky.

Then, on cue, Mom says, "Fly, fight, win!"

And then they hug again, this time slapping each other's backs so hard I can hear their ribs vibrate.

Dad shakes Mr. Fingerlin's hand and that turns into another hug.

"It's been a long time, Ruben. Good to see you!" Mr. Fingerlin says.

Buddy and I just stand there, staring at each other. She's legs-up-to-her-neck, supermodel tall. The sun is beaming down on her, creating a halo around her dark brown braids, matchy-matchy outfit, and sparkly red nail polish.

"This is Annabelle."

I don't look up when Dad says this. I just zoom in on my Converse sneaker-boot, which is untied again. A clear sign that even my shoes want to break free of this place!

"Pleasure to meet you." Mr. Fingerlin shakes my hand firmly. "Wendy and I go way back to our Academy days in Colorado. She was always tougher and smarter than me. And look at her now. Master Sergeant!"

"Thank you for agreeing to meet with us so early, Pete," Mom says.

"No problem. Forgive me. This is Rachael Myers." Mr. Fingerlin points to Buddy girl. She gives a weak smile and shakes all of our hands.

"Look at that! You already have a friend, and the day is just beginning!" Mom's voice is beyond excited.

Great. A forced friendship is just what I need.

"Rachael will show you around before the day starts," Mr. Fingerlin says.

"Mom, Dad, I have it from here. You can leave now. OK?" I say with my teeth pressed together.

"You sure, *schätzchen*?"

"Bless you!" Rachael says to Mom.

"Oh!" Mom chuckles. "I didn't sneeze, dear. I was calling Annabelle my little—"

"Mom!" I cough one time. "I'll see you when I get home."

"Can't wait to hear all about your first day. *Viel glück!*" Mom winks at me.

Rachael's eyebrows rise half an inch.

The back of my neck is burning. I don't respond in German. All I say is, "Bye."

They head toward the exit. Dad walks like a normal human, and of course Mom is walking backward, blowing kisses at me before she disappears out the door.

"Let's get started!" Mr. Fingerlin hands me a folder with my schedule and papers of all the activities McManus has to offer. He explains that Rachael is the president of the Positive Behavior in Schools (PBIS) club and they do character-building activities for the school community.

The more he talks, the more I start to think that PBIS stands for *Practically Babysitting Incoming Students*. I want no part, and, judging by Rachael's lack of enthusiasm, neither does she.

"And now, I'll have Rachael take over. I'll be in my office if you ladies need me." Mr. Fingerlin walks down the hall in the opposite direction.

Rachael starts walking, and I follow.

"Yo," she says, "what in the world did your mom say to you before she left?"

"She wished me good luck."

"You from Russia or something?"

"Germany. But I was born here."

Rachael stops short and whips around. One of her long braids smacks me right in the nose. "They got black people in Germany?"

I knew that was coming. Off base in Germany, sometimes I felt like people stared at me like I was a circus act. I see it's not going to be any different here.

"Well, yeah," I say. "Not a lot of black people, though. Mom's in the Air Force, so we move a lot."

Rachael makes a face that I can't quite read.

Then she grabs my folder and takes a look at my schedule. "All right, I'll make this quick. Hope you're a fast learner." She stops in front of a wall with mini metal doors and locks. "You're number six-one-nine." She points.

I open it and look inside, super confused.

Rachael stares at me. "OMG, they don't have lockers in Germany?" She laughs. "You put your things in there. But you're gonna need a lock for your stuff. We got a few people with sticky fingers around here."

Images of syrupy hands touching my things—especially my MacBook, which I have in my knapsack right now—run through my mind.

"I'm sorry. Why are their fingers sticky?"

Rachael doesn't answer. She just laughs some more and says, "Maybe hold on to your things for today. Have your parents take you to Target to get you a lock."

Maybe they do have lockers in Germany. I wouldn't know because I've been *homeschooled*! But of course I don't tell her that. I just nod my head like, *Totally! I get it!*

Rachael zips around the whole school in what feels like five minutes. Up the stairs and down the stairs, every word coming out faster than the other like she wants to hurry up and get this over with. Cafeteria. Gym. Auditorium—"for useless assemblies." Playground—which looks nothing like what we had in Germany. There's absolutely nothing to play with on these grounds. My homeroom, 201, which is also Rachael's. And the locations of the rest of my classes. By the time we're back at the entrance of the school, I don't remember a thing.

It's official. I want to go home. Now.

Our last stop is the bathroom.

"The bell's gonna ring soon, so I have to put my face on."

I look at Rachael, puzzled. *But your face is on . . . right?* Of course, I don't say that, I just trail inside behind her.

She pulls a fuzzy, pink bag out of her backpack. The next part plays out like a Hollywood glamour short film. Off screen, a fan is blowing. Better yet, there are two people—one at each side—moving gigantic fans up and down. Rachael's braids whip against the wind. The camera zooms in as she starts to umm . . . *put her face on.* Lip gloss. Mascara. Black pencil on her eyelids.

The camera pans right, and the lenses have to refocus when they get to me because apparently my entire outfit is distorting the image. There I am, staring and saying nothing while Rachael transforms herself into Beyoncé's twin. Then, I don't know why, but I start looking at my reflection in the full-length mirror compared to hers: my purple leggings, which are sagging, thanks to the fact that my whole body is made up of parallel lines, compared to her form-fitting, curve-hugging blue jeans. My old, worn-out Converses, compared to her spotless Nike sneakers. My hair, which is playing a game of *Which curl can touch the ceiling first?* compared to hers, which apparently grows downward.

Rachael must think I look ridiculous.

"Want some lip gloss?" Rachael jolts me out of the scene.

I swallow. "No, I'm fine. I left mine at home."

Shopping list for Target: 1. lock 2. lip gloss

"You know, for a black German girl, you speak good English. Like no accent or anything."

The tension in my shoulders loosens a bit. A voice inside whispers, *Play it cool, Annabelle.*

"Well, English is my first language." I hop on the sink counter and lean against the wall. "We moved bases a lot, so I picked up on German. Dad's half Puerto Rican, so he taught me Spanish, and my best friend is Japanese, so she and her dad taught me a little of that too."

I'm almost ready to mention living in the UK. You know, hit her with the good stuff. Show off my impressive British accent. But then I feel my left butt cheek turn wet, and I start to slide off the side of the sink counter.

"Whoa, you OK?" Rachael catches my wrist before I fall.

"Yeah . . . *totally.*" I pull my shirt down to hide the water stain on my butt.

"You're like a walking, breathing globe." Rachael laughs.

Then I start laughing too. And there we are, laughing

together like two *amigas*. Really, I'm not sure if Rachael meant that as a compliment or an insult, but who cares! If only Mom, Dad, and Mae could see me now!

The bell rings, and outside the halls get loud—fast. Rachael tosses her makeup in the pink bag and beelines it for the door. She turns quickly. "Good luck, umm . . . what was your name again?"

My heart plummets to the floor. "Annabelle."

I'm not sure if she hears me, because she's already opening the bathroom door. There's a crowd outside, and they're all waiting for *her*, like the paparazzi. They're taking selfies with Rachael and saying things like:

"You slaying that outfit, girl!"

"Great lip gloss shade, bae!"

"I'll cut off my pinky toe and donate it to science if you sit next to me in homeroom."

OK, the last one might be a stretch. But seriously, this exact scene is why I don't do school.

A couple of super cute guys walk by, smiling and waving at Rachael and company. Meanwhile, I'm standing there, trying to look . . . *down with my bad self*!

"Who's that?" one of her adoring fans asks.

Rachael stops selfie-posing for a split second and says, "Oh, that's just the new kid."

The bell rings, and just like that they all rush to homeroom. Without me.

5

THE DAY GETS BETTER

As I near homeroom, I hear noise and commotion. I take a deep breath and pray that no one notices me so I can quickly find a seat. Here goes nothing.

The chaos stops as soon as I get to the doorway. The whole class is staring at me. If this were a movie, the houselights would dim, and the spotlight would land right on my horrified face.

The teacher stops writing on the board and turns to me. "You must be our new student!"

My whole body turns to ice. I hear a chuckle coming from somewhere, but I can't pinpoint it.

"I'm Mrs. Rodriguez." She walks over and grabs my hand to shake it. "Well, don't just stand there. Come in! Come in!" Mrs. Rodriguez grabs me by the shoulders, walks me inside, and plants me dead smack in front of the room.

I have an audience. Lovely.

"Class, we have a new student!" she says.

I'm dying inside. Slowly. I try my best not to look at anyone, though I see Rachael and company and I feel everyone's eyeballs glued to me.

Mrs. Rodriguez inches her face real close to mine and smiles. She has a smear of red lipstick on her teeth. *Looks like she didn't do a good job putting* her *face on,* I think.

"Go on. Introduce yourself, . . ."—she looks at her roster to double-check my name—"Annabelle."

My eyes find the floor. I whisper, "My name is Annabelle. Annabelle Louis."

"Speak up!" Jerk #1, for $500.

"We can't hear you." Jerk #2, double the money.

"Yo, is she a student or the janitor?" Jerk #3 wins it all!

The whispers spill out. I stay busy looking at the tile patterns on the floor. Red-blue-red-blue and one random black, like they ran out of tiles in that one spot.

Is this over yet?

"She's from Germany, y'all!" It's Rachael. At least she remembered that. There's a small tug in my stomach.

"Is that where she got those kicks from?" someone pipes up. "'Cause I ain't never seen nothing like those in the mall!"

The whole class erupts into talking and laughter.

That's it. I'm never coming back. I don't care if Dad is going back to work. I'll homeschool myself.

"OK, class, that's enough!" Mrs. Rodriguez screams, and that shuts them up. "You may find an empty seat, Annabelle."

I half look up at the desks aligned in perfect, mile-long rows, praying there's a seat right in the front so I can put an end to the museum exhibit that is Annabelle Louis. But nope, *nada*.

"There's one back here!" A smiling kid with a mouth full of braces stands up and beckons me to come join him.

"Ooooh!" someone calls out.

I can't take one more second, so I speed-walk to the back of the room where Brace Face is happily waiting for me. You'd think things couldn't get any worse, but my shoelace decides now is the proper time to find the floor. Again. By the time I realize it, it's too late. My right foot finds the left lace and . . .

TIMBERRRRR!

I go tumbling. My knapsack goes airborne. Brace Face catches it before my pencils, notebooks, and MacBook fall out.

"SAFE!" he yells, holding it up like it's a trophy.

The class is laughing. I'm dying. Brace Face is smiling like he's the king of seventh grade. Mrs. Rodriguez is telling everyone to quiet down so she can take attendance.

I'm definitely going to YouTube some homeschooling videos as soon as I finish setting up my girl cave.

Everyone settles down after attendance. Then Mrs. Rodriguez starts to write some words on the board: SPORTS DAY!

A lot of the kids start cheering.

"Don't forget that Sports Day is next week. Who would like to stand up, introduce themselves, and tell Annabelle what that means?" Mrs. Rodriguez looks around the room hopefully.

Brace Face doesn't waste a second. He bolts out of his seat and squares his shoulders. "Hello, Annabelle. My name is Johnathan Lopez, but you can call me John. Welcome to McManus! Sports Day is cool because for one whole day, all of our academic classes are replaced by sports. We get to check out the different sports that McManus has to offer. Everybody gets a chance to play. That'll help you decide if you want to try out for a team. Personally, I've got my eyes on the swim team."

Two students clap. A girl and a boy seated in front of us.

John takes a bow and then flashes me a shiny smile.

"Excellent! Thank you, Johnathan," Mrs. Rodriguez says. "I'm going to pass around a list of what you'll need to bring for each activity."

Mrs. Rodriguez walks around passing out our

individual Sports Day assignments. "We had to place you where we could, since you joined us a little late," she says when she reaches me.

I take the paper and stuff it into my knapsack. Doesn't matter anyway because I won't be here by next Wednesday.

John leans toward me and asks, "What sports did you get?"

I don't even look at him as I shrug.

"Don't worry. The day gets better, Annabelle. Promise."

The bell rings. I toss my knapsack over my shoulder and get out of there as fast as I can.

6

TEXTING FROM BASE

Mom: *Schätzchen! Mi amor!* My love! I'm working a double shift, so can't talk on the phone. BUT TEXT ME ABOUT YOUR FIRST DAY! <3

Fifteen minutes later . . .

Mom: Annabelle, you there?

Mom to Group, Belle, Dad: Ruben, please don't tell me you forgot to pick our daughter up from school!

Dad to Group, Belle, Mom: I picked her up . . . on time. She's locked away in her girl cave. She won't talk to me.

Mom to Group, Belle, Dad: Annabelle, we'll talk about everything as soon as I get home. OK, sweetie?

Three hours later . . .

Belle to Group, Mom, Dad: There's nothing to talk about. Effective immediately, I'm dropping out of middle school.

7

DAPHNE DOESN'T

Me and my big mouth! (Or should I say fingers.)

As soon as I clicked send, my parents sprung into action. Mom left work early, sped up the highway, and hit me with a lecture as soon as she got home: *There shall be no dropping out of anything, young lady. Not when I busted my butt getting three degrees! We don't do failure in this family!*

Needless to say, I've been carrying out my sentence at McManus Middle School ever since. And to make things a little more interesting, Mom thought it would be a good idea for me to see a therapist.

So here I am pacing the wooden floors in the doctor's office, puzzled by the googly-eyed horse heads protruding from the walls. There are four of them, half black, half brown hair sticking out in mid-air, staring me down like I'm hiding a carrot in my back pocket. And they don't look too happy right about now. That makes five of us.

Still in uniform, Mom is seated on a leather couch next to large double windows.

Dr. Varma walks in with a gigantic smile and caked-on makeup that's way too pale for her brown skin.

"Pleasure to meet you, Master Sergeant Louis. Thank you for your service."

Mom rises and shakes Dr. Varma's hand. "Pleasure's all mine."

"And this must be Annabelle?"

"Hi." I keep my eyes on her wedge sandals.

"Ah, she's shy, I see," Dr. Varma says, like she's known me my whole life. "*Herzlich willkommen*. Welcome!"

"*Danke!*" I thank her, surprised to be feeling a little more relaxed now. "You speak German?"

"My dad served in Germany, like your mum. And in the UK and Japan too. We moved around quite a bit, just like you. I bet you know a few different languages."

Three years in Japan, two and a half years a piece in Spain and the UK, and five years in Germany will do that.

"Oh, I speak a bit of this and that," I say, shrugging.

Dr. Varma asks Mom to sit in the waiting room while we talk. Then she tells me to take a seat on the couch.

"Annabelle, what are your thoughts about your mum bringing you to see a therapist?"

I scan my brain for the right response. On more than

a few occasions, I've heard Mom and Dad speak in whispered words:

Annabelle is so . . . shy.

Maybe all the moving is affecting her.

She just needs to make friends.

Dr. Varma tips her head as though I'm taking too long to answer.

"My thoughts are . . . that I don't need a therapist. No offense. Isn't this where people go when they're going crazy?"

"No, not exactly," Dr. Varma says. "Sometimes when there are big changes in a family, like your recent move to the United States, it's good to meet with a therapist to help you understand and make a plan for your new life."

I'm not sure what she wants me to do with that, so I just sit there silently.

"Tell me about life at McManus!" Dr. Varma says that like it's the greatest thing ever.

I chew on my bottom lip.

"You know, we could sit here for the hour and do nothing, though I'm sure your mum won't be happy about that. Consider this a place where you can empty out all of your feelings and nothing will ever leave this room. Now, go on, tell me about your new school. It can't be *that* bad," Dr. Varma says.

You don't know the half of it, lady, I think, and then I let it all fly. "I've been a student at McManus Middle School for one week and so far I've"—I tick them off on my fingers as I speak—"forgotten my locker combination twice. Thrown out my nasty lunch three times. Gotten lost four times. And last, but not least, tossed my favorite pair of Converses in the trash."

Dr. Varma is writing nonstop, but pauses to gnaw on her pen eraser. "Why'd you throw away your shoes?" she asks.

I don't feel like reliving the memory and the stares. "They're just not my style anymore," I say, looking down at my black leather Mary Janes. The real reason was that Rachael and everyone else was looking at my sneakers like they were from outer space.

"Interesting." Dr. Varma starts scribbling again.

"Why do you do that?"

"Do what?" Dr. Varma's eyes are intensely fixed on her notepad.

"Write all of this stuff down . . . like I'm some kind of experiment?"

She stops writing, looks up, and smiles. "Tell me. In a perfect world, what would your life be like?"

"I don't know. I'd be back home in Germany, or even better, back in the UK. That's where my best friend, Mae, lives. And Mom would be retired already, so no more moving." Thinking about that makes my shoulders instantly relax.

"My job is to help you find a support system, to get you through this move and the time your mum will be gone," Dr. Varma says.

We sit there for a few moments silently. I gaze out the big windows next to the couch. Outside there are kids riding bikes, cars driving by, the whole Earth moving along. Meanwhile, my old life and my best friend are on another continent.

"Mum tells me you're a techie and you make great videos. I would love to see your work one day," Dr. Varma says.

"I can show you now, if you'd like."

Dr. Varma claps her hands. "Absolutely!"

I grab my MacBook out of my knapsack, open it up, click on the iMovie app, and show her a few clips on full-screen mode. The first one is a really old voiceover of me acting out an epic Lego battle. The other is a voiceover of me re-enacting the human-eating plant scene from my favorite movie, *Little Shop of Horrors*. Fake screams and all. That one sends Dr. Varma into a fit of laughter.

Most of my videos are short, not even lasting a full minute. I show Dr. Varma four of them, and she applauds after each one. Then she starts to pick up her notepad, but stops herself. "You have such a talent, Annabelle!"

"Oh, it's no big deal. Just stuff I like to do in my spare time when I'm in my girl cave."

"It's interesting how you used the word experiment earlier. And while I certainly don't think *you* are an experiment, watching your videos made me think of one. How about we forget the notepads and do something totally different?"

Now this lady's got my attention. "OK," I say, "what do you have in mind?"

"Clearly, your parents love you, and I can tell that you are a close-knit family. All those years braving new countries together, constantly moving, all you've ever had were each other. And just when you thought things were settling down, your mum and dad send you off into the wilderness! No wonder you told them you wanted to drop out of school!"

Yes! Finally, someone gets it!

"To be fair, they just want you to break out of your shyness and make new friends. And really, that's why I'm here, Annabelle. To help you come up with some strategies. But I think you just proved that it would be better if you're in control of this whole—for lack of a better word—*experiment*."

Control. Yes, I like that.

"So, how about you start a vlog?"

My eyes widen. OK. That's tech talk. Now she's

speaking my language. "I'm listening," I say, loosening my crossed legs.

"You can use those movie-making skills and create a YouTube channel that features all of your vlogs."

I spring up off the couch, beyond excited. "THAT would be amazing!"

Dr. Varma jumps up with me and blurts: "You can try out some of the activities that they have at school and then vlog about them. Oh, you're going to be a natural in front of the camera, Annabelle!"

Whoa. Stop it right there.

"I'm sorry. What did you say?" I'm no longer jumping.

Dr. Varma still is, though. Her hair has released from its bun, falling in layers around her shoulders. She's having a party all by herself. Even the horses are looking at her like she's lost it.

"Did I say something wrong?" Dr. Varma snaps out of it.

I plop onto the leather couch, the cushions sighing right along with me. "It's just that I'm used to being *behind* the camera. Not in front of it. My voice is on some of the videos, but I never, ever show my face."

"Why do you think that is?" she asks.

"I don't know. Maybe because, I would feel,"—I search for the right word—"*exposed.*"

"Ah, I see. But you know, it would be such a waste not to use this special skill to help you feel more comfortable in social situations. There has to be a way to compromise."

I scan my brain for how I could make that happen. Maybe it would work, but if only I could . . .

Ding! Ding! Ding! Dr. Varma's timer goes off.

"Saved by the bell!" I spring up off the couch. "Guess that means I'll be leaving."

"Not so fast, young lady. My next appointment isn't for another thirty minutes, and I saw that idea bubbling! I'm going to bring in Mum to discuss this further. We're on to something big here!"

Dr. Varma peeks her head into the waiting room. "May we see you for a moment, Sergeant Louis?"

Mom walks in and takes a seat next to me.

Dr. Varma tells her about how wonderful our intro session was, and then she looks at me. "Annabelle will tell you the rest."

I explain everything to Mom, and she looks really into the whole vlog idea. "But *if* I'm going to make a vlog," I say, "I have some conditions. First, the videos will be marked private. No one sees them except you guys, Dad, and Mae."

"Sounds easy," Dr. Varma cuts me off. "I'm no good with social media, but I'm sure you know what to do."

"Second, I won't use my real name for the vlog."

"Then what name will you use?" Mom asks.

"My middle name, Daphne. No one calls me that anyway."

Dr. Varma and Mom look at each other and nod.

"And third, even though the videos will be private, I refuse to be in front of the camera without some sort of disguise."

Mom laughs at that one. "Well, why would you want to go and do that?"

"I would die if I'm caught, Mom!"

"How dramatic!" Mom says. "OK, costumes, makeup, maybe even a wig. Oh, this will be fun! I know the perfect place I can take you."

"Sounds like a fabulous plan, Annabelle," Dr. Varma says. "Now let's talk about what school activities you'll vlog about."

"Why can't I just vlog about stuff I see on television and in the news?" I ask.

"Let's take what you love—making movies—and pair that with what we want to help you with, which is making friends at school."

"I saw on the school website that next week is Sports Day," Mom says. Then she starts to tell Dr. Varma all about it.

The imaginary camera zooms in on me, and I

explode into a pile of ashes. "I don't do sports," I blurt out. Especially when I had already cooked up the perfect excuse to be absent for Sports Day: food poisoning.

"Oh, but this is a fantastic way to start your vlog!" Dr. Varma says.

Mom gets all excited and says, "Ooh, and I have a great name for it—*Daphne Does It All*! Your first episode will be all about sports and how much *I know* you'll love them!"

I picture myself in a uniform, sweating and trying to throw a ball around.

No thank you.

I force a smile so hard, my cheeks hurt. I don't say anything to Mom because if I recall correctly, Dr. Varma said I am in control. So I come up with the perfect name for my channel: *Daphne DOESN'T*. As in does nothing. Because I think everything about school and extracurricular activities is a waste of my time. None of this will bring Mae back, and there's not a sport in the world that'll keep me from missing Mom when she leaves. And why should I get attached to anything here in Linden? I bet Mom will decide not to retire and we'll end up moving in less than a year.

Right there, I make a decision. Instead of using the vlog to try new activities and make new friends at school, I'll prove how useless they all are in the first place.

That'll show Mom and Dad that I was right all along: homeschooling is a better choice for me.

While Mom and Dr. Varma sit there making plans, I'm drawing up my own for my first episode: "Daphne Definitely Doesn't Do Sports"!

8

HELLO, DAPHNE!

"Where are we going?" I ask as Mom hooks a left into Aviation Plaza. It's the largest outdoor shopping center I've ever seen.

"I think you're going to love this place. It'll bring back some memories." Mom pulls into a parking space.

We walk to the stores. She stops in front of a store called Second Chance. In the display window, there's a mannequin wearing a vintage dress that looks straight from the Elizabethan era. Another mannequin looks like a detective with a long trench coat. And there's a rack full of jewelry from different parts of the world.

I am IN LOVE!

"Oh my goodness, Mom, this is like . . ." My skin gets all tingly just thinking about it.

"Trödelei!" Mom and I sing the word together.

A random couple walk past us and twist their faces.

Trödelei is this little thrift store in Berlin. Right

outside of it is a stand that sells hot, fresh crepes filled with Nutella and topped with ice cream. Mom would take me there whenever she came back from a TDY. Typically, those assignments were short. Two weeks in Austria or a week in Denmark while Dad and I stayed on base in Germany.

Post-TDY was our special time. Just the two of us roaming the streets of downtown Berlin, rummaging through the most unique items at Trödelei, and going to the park afterward.

"Ready to get Daphne-fied?" Mom asks.

"Oh yeah!"

The movie in my head begins. *Cue music! Lights! Camera! Action!*

We swing open the door . . . annnnnd there isn't a soul here. Any second now, I'm expecting tumbleweeds to roll by.

Houselights down. Cameras off. Better yet, just unplug the whole set.

Second Chance is nearly double the size of Trödelei. How can people just walk by all of this fabulous stuff? For cheap too! In Trödelei, you'd be lucky to have an aisle to yourself. Even still, that would only last a minute.

"Come in! Come in!" A woman with waist-long blond hair scurries over to us. She sounds so excited. I'm pretty sure we're her first customers of the day . . . and judging by how dark it's getting outside, we'll probably be her last.

"Welcome to my store. I'm the owner, Georgia."

"Thank you," Mom says. "I'm Wendy, and this is my daughter, Annabelle."

"Is there anything in particular you're looking for today?" Georgia asks.

"Well, Annabelle is working on . . ." Mom starts talking, and I kind of zone out looking at all the cool things in the store. A Harry Potter-style cloak. A collection of neon and glitter wigs. Feather boas. Old Hollywood wall art. I can see myself dressed as a Victorian duchess or even a British spy! All of this stuff is perfect for my vlog and for decorating my girl cave. Shut up and take ALL of my money!

Mom's rambling breaks me out of my zone. ". . . so she'll need to dress up in different outfits for her online show."

"What did you say?"

Mom is *forever* telling my business. First Dr. Varma. Now the thrift shop lady.

"I was telling Georgia all about your show."

"Online?" Sweet Georgia smiles so wide, her top dentures come undone. "You're gonna be on one of those new types of television? What do they call it, Halo?"

Hulu.

"Nothing on television, ma'am. This is a project . . . for school." I press my finger into Mom's back.

Mom gives me a look that says, *OK, I'll shut up.*

"Well, help yourself, ladies," Georgia says. "We have plenty of goodies!"

Mom and I spend the next hour in Second Chance trying on everything and filling up two carts to bring Daphne and my girl cave to life.

When we get home, we order dinner—Two Tony's makes *the* best Margherita pizza—and get right to work decorating the room where all of the Daphne magic will happen. Two hours later, the girl cave is complete, and it's everything I've ever dreamed of. A real place to call my own.

"Don't stay up too late, *Daphne*," Dad says before heading upstairs to his room.

"I won't, Dad."

"Hope you like your new room, sweetie. And remember to try your best tomorrow. Don't be shy. Just have a good time." Mom kisses my forehead and follows Dad up the basement stairs.

I sit in my girl cave, thinking about how awesome it is. There's film strip art on the walls; a little kitchenette full of soda pop, chips, and Twizzlers; a brand-new camera with a tripod; bright lights; my desk with two screens, my private YouTube channel all set up and ready to go. But even with all these cool things surrounding me, I feel incomplete.

My phone buzzes, and then I know exactly who's missing.

Mae: Good luck tomorrow . . . "Daphne."

9

SPORTS DAY

John walks into homeroom, all smiles. Right away, I notice he's wearing cleats . . . with no cleats (cleatless cleats?), basketball shorts, and a football jersey. Annnnd for good measure, a helmet's sticking out of his backpack. Not that I should talk, with my no-name sneakers, baggy sweats, and hot cocoa–stained T-shirt.

"I got a joke for you," John says, sitting down next to me.

Here we go.

"Why did the football coach go to the bank?"

I'm sure John can see how thrilled I am, so he finishes the joke for me. "He wanted his quarter back!" John laughs so hard his entire body shakes.

"Good one," I say softly.

"Let me see your schedule," he says.

I pull it out of my notebook and hand him the paper of doom: lacrosse, football, and swim.

"Nice! You picked the same sports I did."

"Not really. They stuck me wherever because I started school late."

Rachael arrives to homeroom fashionably late. Everything she's wearing is matchy-matchy princess perfect. And so begin the comments from her fans. . . .

Fan #1: "Are those the newest Adidas?"

Rachael: "Oh, these? They haven't hit the stores yet."

Fan #2: "Love the makeup today, girl!"

Rachael: "Oh, this? Just some waterproof mascara and cherry bomb ChapStick."

Every. Single. Boy. In class drools on the floor. Except John. The kid marches to the beat of his own drum.

The bell rings, and I make my way to the field out back.

"Wait up, Annabelle." John runs to catch up to me.

A whistle blows hard and loud from the field. "Hurry!" the teacher yells. "We have a lot to learn."

Twenty-one of us surround the teacher and his whiteboard full of drawings that look like hieroglyphics to me. Xs, Os, and lines are scribbled everywhere.

"Welcome to lacrosse! I'm Coach Carmine." He points to the teachers standing beside him. "This is your referee, Mr. Thomas, your umpire, Mrs. Locke, and your field judge, Mr. Williams. Now, who here has played lacrosse before?"

Every. Single. Hand. Goes up. Lovely.

And cue single focus zoom!

Of course everyone turns around and looks at me.

"So you're new to lacrosse, eh?" Coach Carmine smirks.

"She's new to this whole country!" someone calls out.

"I was born here but moved overseas when I was really young." I want to say all of that loud and proud enough to prove the point that I *am* American, but everything comes out in a whisper.

"Where did you move from?" Coach asks.

"Germany." My entire face is fixed on the grass. *And the UK. And Spain. And Japan. And apparently everywhere else but here!*

"No lacrosse in Germany, I imagine," Coach says.

I shake my head. Not that I would know.

"We'll go easy on you, then," he says, trying to make me feel better.

Coach gives us a rundown of everything we need to know about the sport. How to scoop the ball. How to catch the ball in the pocket. All the infringements—and the list is long. The equipment. The history. None of it sticks in my brain beyond the cool fact that lacrosse was invented by Native Americans, though Coach Carmine can't remember which specific tribe.

Mrs. Locke passes out all the equipment to the players and then turns her attention to me. She outfits me with full gear—helmet, shoulder guards, arm pads, gloves, and a netted stick—and positions me in front of the "goal crease" while the other teachers separate everyone into teams of ten.

I start thinking up an escape plan. Maybe I could say I have to go to the bathroom and stay there until the game is over? But how would I get all of this equipment off by myself? And what would everyone think of me being in the bathroom for the entire game? Ugh!

"Relax. This will be fun." Mrs. Locke sees my panic through the helmet.

"All you have to do is try to stop the opposing team from scoring. That's it!"

Sure, lady. Sounds easy.

Mrs. Locke runs off and takes her spot as umpire.

Mr. Thomas screams, "Are you ready? PLAY!" He blows a whistle, and all chaos breaks loose.

The kids prance about with their nets in the air, running after this teeny-tiny ball as it dances around the field. If I didn't know any better, I'd think they were chasing butterflies. All that's missing are sunflowers, a rainbow in the sky, and Taylor Swift playing on repeat. It is the funniest thing I've seen in weeks. Laughter boils inside me, and all of a sudden I'm hunched over, completely unaware of the ball that's just landed smack into the goal.

The opposing team roars!

"Wake up, Annabelle!" one of the kids on my team calls out.

That wipes the smile right off my face.

John runs over to me. "Don't worry about him. Just try your best to block the ball from going in. This will be over before you know it."

Easy for him to say.

Ladies and gentlemen, I present the pleasant sounds of the next three quarters:

Smack!
Ouch!
Whoops!
Oof!

A performance of grand measure, featuring the one, the only . . . Annabelle Louis!

Coach Carmine blows the whistle. Game over. The score is . . . 8 to 0.

"Nice job, Annabelle!"

"Yeah, thanks for nothing!"

I can't get out of this stupid lacrosse *costume* fast enough. I hate lacrosse. I hate this school. I hate moving. I hate TDY. I zip across the field, tears flying in the wind, but you-know-who is already following me inside.

"Wait up!" John has a friend with him. "Where are you going?" he asks.

"To the bathroom . . . for the rest of the day," I mutter.

We stand in the empty cafeteria, silent for a few seconds, until girl-with-the-friendly-smile speaks. "Don't be silly! You can't hang out in there. Teachers will mark you as 'cut' and then you'll have bigger problems than lacrosse."

I stare at my shoes, wondering if it'd be worth it.

"I'm Clairna, by the way."

I notice her eyes are friendly too. A deep, warm brown, just like Mom's.

"Nice to meet you, but I'm not doing any of the other sports. This is just—"

"Not your thing?" Clairna tilts her head. "I hate Sports Day too. Most of *our kind* do."

"What's that supposed to mean—our kind?" I ask.

"Oh, come on," John begins. "All schools have their cliques. There's the popular clique."

"And the jock clique!" Clairna chimes in.

"Oh yeah, and the artsy clique," I add, remembering the kids at the lunch table who were building chicken nugget sculptures the other day.

We all laugh.

"And then there's . . . us." Clairna gets all serious. "The not-so-athletic, totally unpopular, unfashionable clique."

"Speak for yourself, Clairna. I always rock the latest gear." John points to his cleatless cleats, and we start laughing all over again.

"Don't beat yourself up. For what it's worth, our whole team sucked," Clairna says.

"Football is next. Come on, you're not gonna miss that, are you?" John does a macho man pose.

"I promise it will be fun . . . and funny." Clairna chuckles.

I chew on my inner cheek. Maybe she's right. At least I *do* know what football is—even though they say it funny here in the States. Dad and I pronounce it *fútbol*. Every four years, Dad watches the World Cup and cheers for Brazil. Five wins is nothing to sneeze at.

"OK, I'll do it."

"Cool!" Clairna does a little happy dance. By the time we reach the front of McManus, we've already missed the bus to Tiger Stadium. Mr. Fingerlin is directing students to other activities.

"Very late, I see." Mr. Fingerlin gives us the *tsk-tsk* voice.

"We had to stop at the bathroom," John says.

"You guys can catch this one." Mr. Fingerlin taps the door of bus number 634.

We climb on, and a few streetlights and turns later, the bus pulls up and we run onto the sidelines. A game is already in progress. According to the scoreboard, the score is 7–6, and they are in the final stretch.

What a relief! Now we won't have to play. The teacher will just mark our names on the attendance list. And now I can get this God-awful part of this day over with.

"Lopez, Joseph, new kid—you're late!" the coach yells as we run to the bench.

"Coach Tillman, this is Annabelle Louis." John uses my full name like it matters.

"Quick! Joseph, Lopez, play defense." Coach Tillman sounds like Darth Vader from Star Wars.

Clairna and John run to the field, slapping their helmets on.

"Louis, I'm gonna have you substitute kick for a field goal," he explains. "Twenty yards. Get 'em."

He hands me a helmet, taps me on the shoulder, and my whole body goes flying toward the field. My legs are running and so is my brain. Field goal? Kick the ball? Everyone is staring at me, and I'm having flashbacks to the first day all over again.

There's a triangular device holding the ball. It doesn't

look anything like what I've seen in the World Cup. Four years is a long time. Maybe they changed the style of the ball?

I throw John a look, and he mutters through his helmet, "Just kick and we run it to the end, I guess?"

Coach Tillman blows his whistle.

I take a deep breath, my eyes on the brown, pointy-looking ball. I swing my right foot back, and BAM! The ball goes soaring, kids are screaming, "Whoa!" And I! Feel! Amazing!

As soon as the ball hits the ground, I gain speed right behind it and start kicking and running at the same time. And I'm moving it fast too! The ball isn't moving like it does in the World Cup. It's wobbling, really, like it's heavier than the average *fútbol*.

Kids are gaining on me, and I can hear them screaming:

"What is she doing?"

"This is hilarious!"

"This ain't soccer!"

Finally the ball passes the white line. That means I scored for my team, right? Take that, haters! I jump and spin around, my fists pumping to the sky. Several students are laughing and rolling on the ground. And suddenly my stomach begins eating itself. Clairna and John run over to me.

"I think you were playing a different sport, Annabelle," Clairna says.

"But he said drive it to the line, or something like that . . . right?"

And cue sweat beads!

The kids are still rolling, and Coach Tillman is running our way. "That was something else, kid," he says. Then he yells at everyone on the ground. "Get up, show's over. Get to lunch!"

Apparently, I was playing *fútbol* . . . as in soccer. Not as in *American* football.

I
AM
AN
IDIOT!

There's no way I'm getting on that bus where every single teammate is waiting to finish making fun of me. Coach Tillman agrees to let Clairna, John, and me wait for a later bus.

* * *

By the time we get back to McManus, there are fifteen minutes left to eat lunch. While Clairna and John head to the cafeteria, I tell them that I brought lunch from home and I have to grab it from my locker.

Which is a lie.

I find an empty janitor's closet. It's not my girl

cave, and even though I'm surrounded by buckets of dirty mop water and a couple of rat traps, it'll do. I pull out a granola bar from my knapsack and text Mae.

Me: That's it. I quit. And I mean it this time.

Mae: Hey, *amiga*! What happened?

Me: Sports happened.

Mae: :(

Me: I'm not going to the last class. Faking sick and going to the nurse. Excuse? Food poisoning. Easy to believe when today's lunch is dog food dressed up as something called a sloppy joe.

Mae: Good excuse! Bad lunch! What's your last sport?

Me: Swim. And don't you even think about it!

Mae: But you swim so fast! Remember all the times you beat me on holiday in the Dominican Republic?

Just then, there's a loud bang on the door.

Me: Gotta go. Janitor alert.

Mae: <3

"Annabelle, we know you're in there." It's Clairna.

"How did you find me?" I whisper through the crack.

"You're not the first seventh grader to hide in here on a bad day."

I undo the lock and open the door. John and Clairna walk in, followed by another kid.

And he doesn't look too happy. "It stinks in here," he says. "Why would you hide in the janitor's closet when there's the paper supply closet just two doors down?"

John takes a deep breath. "I love the smell of paper."

Clairna claps. "Focus, people. Annabelle, Navdeep. Navdeep, Annabelle."

"Just call me Nav."

"Um, hi, Nav," I say softly.

Clairna gives Nav a rundown of how awfully embarrassing lacrosse and football were.

Thanks for telling all of my business, Clairna!

But Nav doesn't laugh one bit. In fact, he looks like he . . . understands.

"My family moved here from India when I was in fifth grade. They just plopped me in school with a bunch of kids who made fun of my English and the way I dressed and the lunch I'd bring from home. And sports? Forget it! I knew nothing about American football or lacrosse."

Every single word makes me feel better. Sort of. But it won't make this day end any sooner.

"I can't go to swim class," I announce.

"This is happening." Clairna marches me out of the janitor's closet.

The four of us walk past the main office and straight out the front doors. The Linden YMCA bus is waiting to take a group of us to the last activity of the day.

Mr. Fingerlin is waiting outside. "Swim classes will be held separately for boys and girls!" he announces, and I'm not sure if I'm relieved (because the thought of being in my bathing suit in front of boys is enough to make me vomit) or nervous (because John has been with me all day, helping me get through this nightmare). But Clairna will be there, so that helps.

Out of the blue, I feel someone staring at me. It's Rachael. She looks at me for a microsecond and then turns forward.

The bus doors open. Rachael goes on first and her adoring fans follow.

Clairna and I grab a seat in the back of the bus. For the next ten minutes, we're stuck listening to Rachael and friends sing about making money moves and wearing expensive shoes that are red on the bottom.

"It's hip-hop," Clairna says. "You like?"

I smile and nod.

The bus pulls up to the Linden YMCA, and we're led straight to the locker room to change into our swimsuits. That's when I realize I've made the biggest mistake of my life: letting Mom pack my bag for me.

Strike 1: She forgot my swim cap. My hair will hate me for this.

Strike 2: The swimsuit she's picked has ducks on it . . . DUCKS!!!! And I haven't worn it in, I don't know, YEARS!!!!

Meanwhile, Rachael looks like a supermodel in her red, white, and blue striped tankini.

A loud whistle sounds from outside. "File in line, ladies, and let's get to work!"

As we get in line, one of Rachael's friends—the one with a fake smile and an extra side of drool, special just for Rachael—says, "Love the ducks, Annabelle. Slay, girl, *slay!*"

And cue laughter!

Clairna pinches me as a reminder: *Block it out, girl.*

The pool at the YMCA is massive, Olympic size.

Coach Hewitt reviews three techniques with us: breaststroke, forward stroke, and backstroke. Surprisingly, I know how to do them all. No fumbles. No weird laughter. Finally I am not the center of attention.

"And now, for a little bit of friendly competition, let's have a race for the butterfly stroke!" Coach Hewitt announces.

The girls cheer. I deflate. Fast.

She splits us up, and surprise, surprise! Rachael is my partner.

Clairna is two girls ahead of me. Coach Hewitt blows her whistle. Clairna jumps in the water and starts swimming for her life. But by the time Clairna reaches one end, her competitor is already circling back.

The line moves up swiftly, and it's finally my turn. Coach begins the countdown. Rachael and I bend our knees in three, two, one . . . blast off!

My legs don't stop for one second. Memories of old times swim in my mind: Mae and me racing each other in the hotel pool in the Dominican Republic. Our two families brought together by the Air Force. Bonded forever. All of it makes me miss her. I push faster, harder. My hand touches the pool wall. I do a flip under the water, press my feet against the wall and swim to the other side, my hair flailing all around me. When I touch the starting wall and lift my head above the water, Coach is blowing the whistle and Clairna is screaming, "Oh my God, you won!"

I did? I want to shout. I want to jump. I want to pump my fist to the sky. This day didn't turn out so bad after all!

Rachael shakes my hand and says, "Congratulations." We get out of the pool, and before I can reach my towel, it happens. I knew it was coming. My hair becomes a leafy bush. My swimsuit is so small that the ducks on my butt have disappeared and become the biggest wedgie known to man!

"Might be time for a new swimsuit," Coach Hewitt whispers softly, so no one hears.

But a couple of girls are already laughing at me, and I'm not sure if it's because of the massive wedgie or the fact that my hair is slowly turning into an oak tree.

10

VLOG

As soon as I get home, I take a shower, change, and head straight to my girl cave in the basement. I'm itching to do my first vlog, and I know exactly what I'm going to say.

First, I have to transform myself into Daphne.

I keep repeating the word "flashy" over and over in my head. I find a silver sequin shirt with bell-shaped sleeves and a neon green feather boa. I add the hot pink framed glasses, and the finishing touch is the wig— straight, long, and orange. My whole outfit is so ugly, it's perfect!

Mom even got me some makeup so I can go the extra mile and *put my face on*. So I apply a light pink lip gloss and rose-tinted blush. If only Rachael could see me now!

When I look in the mirror, I don't even recognize myself.

Hello, Daphne! Let's do this!

I set up the tripod in front of my chair, flash on the

lights, and click the record button on the video camera. At first I sit there and don't say anything. My stomach feels funny. I can't do this. Why am I chickening out of this thing?

I whip out my cell phone and let my fingers fly.

Me: That's it, I quit! I don't do sports and apparently I can't even make this vlog.

For the next ten minutes, I pace the room contemplating the meaning of life and waiting for Mae to respond.

Mae: Sorry, was watching the tele. No excuses, Annabelle. Just be yourself. Make the video. It's not like anyone is watching it . . . well, except ME! I can't wait. Now, go on!

Ugh! She's right. This is just an experiment. What's the worst that could happen?

I start over and hit the record button. My shoulders loosen up, I think back on every terrible part of Sports Day and why everything about sports is plain awful. Like magic, the words start coming out. And I'm not sure why, but I'm speaking in a British accent.

"Hey, what's up, guys? It's Daphne, and welcome to my social experiment. Today's vlog is entitled 'Daphne *Definitely* Doesn't Do Sports'!

"I'll be talking to you about the top five things I hate about sports:

"Number one: Too many rules. Throw the ball, catch it, kick it. Touch the pool wall with one hand. Don't hold the ball longer than four seconds in the goal crease. How about . . . no?

"Number two: Spaghetti arms. If you are like me—shapeless, made of parallel lines and noodle arms—sports will never, ever be a good thing!

"Number three: Getting it wrong in front of everyone and having them laugh at you.

"Number four: It's dirty outside. Why would anyone want to play where there's mud and bugs?

"Number five: Last but not least . . . everything. No, seriously. The sweat. The growling. The falling. The water up your nose. The wedgies. It's all awful!

"So there you have it! The top five things I hate about sports and why I will NEVER do them again. My mum wanted me to give sports a real effort because, according to her, 'you can make friends.' And I did make a couple today. Sort of. But still, this sports thing is not for me. Thank you for watching this video! Leave a comment if you wish! Or not."

When I'm done recording, I import the video to iMovie and start editing. I add in a few animation effects. Mud flying. Spaghetti splatting against the screen and sliding down to a slow death.

By the time I'm done with everything, I'm itching to

show everyone. But Dad is asleep, Mom's at Fort Dix, and it's three in the morning in the UK. I decide to leave the video public for a bit so Mae can see it. I send her a text.

> **Me**: Just uploaded my first vlog. It's public, so hurry up and watch. Eeep!

I wait a few minutes, hoping that she's up reading and will text me back. But she doesn't.

UGH!

11

BUSTED!

When I wake up the next morning, there are parts of me hurting that I never even knew could hurt. Really, my toenails? Getting dressed is a slow and painful process. Even chewing my breakfast hurts.

Dad screams, "You're going to be late, Annabelle! And I have a train to catch. Let's go!"

I shuffle to grab my school things, and then we zoom out the door and hit the road.

I get to homeroom with just a minute to spare.

"Why are you walking like that?" Rachael asks.

"Oh, no reason." But on the inside I'm saying, "BECAUSE SPORTS DAY NEARLY KILLED ME!"

We're not allowed to have cell phones in class, but today I break the rules because Mae still hasn't texted me back and I'm dying to know what she thinks of my vlog.

Third period, I have computer class. The class size

is pretty large, and when the teacher isn't looking, I check my phone.

> **Mae**: So sorry for the late reply. Nasty cold. Fever all night. But I just watched your video, and HOLY MOLY 46 views? I thought you were keeping it private?

I feel like screaming through the phone: *HELLO! I left it public for you, but you took too long and now how many people have seen it????*

Forty-six views? Every organ in my digestive system seems to squeeze into one giant mass.

Mrs. Gironda starts her lesson on Microsoft Excel, which is a joke because I already know it. Comes with the territory when your dad is a tech genius.

I don't have time to listen to this. I need to log into my YouTube account ASAP and change the privacy setting. We're not allowed to go on YouTube or any social media during class, so I have to do it from my phone . . . which I'm not supposed to have. I click on the link, go to my channel, and see that I no longer have 46 views. I have 98!!!!! And there are comments:

CousinHilary1996: This is hilarious!

ItsACaliThing: Omg I hate sports too!

BossGirl13: When will you post your next vlog?

I need a towel to wipe the sweat off my hands . . . and EVERY SINGLE PART OF ME!

How could this happen? I don't even know how I'm supposed to feel right now. Upset? Proud?

I smell Mrs. Gironda before she even speaks. Mentholated cough drops with a dash of vanilla-scented perfume.

"Annabelle Louis? Please tell me you're not playing on your phone in class."

BUSTED!

"I'm sorry. I was just putting it away."

"Rules are rules, young lady. Hand it over."

The whole class is staring at me now. John shakes his head as if to say, "Just give in."

I hand my phone to Mrs. Gironda.

"You can have it back at the end of the day."

I decide that I will just go to my locker to grab my MacBook during lunch. Then I can make my account private.

The bell rings, and I hurry to my locker. That's when I realize I LEFT MY MACBOOK AT HOME! And I can't even log into my account on someone else's phone because I don't remember the password. Because it's saved on my phone! And my laptop!

It's official. MY LIFE IS RUINED!

After I eat my lunch, Navdeep, Clairna, John, and

I go outside for some fresh air. Navdeep pulls out his phone and starts taking Snapchat pictures.

Clairna's phone beeps with a notification. She checks it and starts giggling.

"What's so funny?" John asks.

"YouTube always sends alerts of new videos that they recommend for me. I've never heard of this channel, but check it out."

I'm standing next to John when she hands him the phone.

And drumroll, please . . .

I see myself pop up on the screen, and I ALMOST DIE!

"Isn't that funny?" John asks, cracking up. He doesn't even flinch when he sees my face and then Daphne's.

In fact, none of them do. They don't recognize that it's me . . . At. All. The disguises and the accent worked. But still, my insides flip-flop around and I feel my face get hot. I have to hurry up and get my phone back before this goes any further.

Later on, when the dismissal bell rings, I zip to Mrs. Gironda's room. The door is locked, and there's a sign on it:

SICK—WENT HOME EARLY!

This has to be a cruel joke. Kids are walking down

the hall. I see them on their phones, hear *my* British accent coming from *their* speakers.

"This Daphne chick needs to make another video." A kid passes by and looks at me as he says this.

Instinctively, both of my hands rise to cover my face. HOW DID THIS HAPPEN? Five billion videos on YouTube and they find mine?

I process that for a second. If they knew it was me, Annabelle Louis, in the video, would they still feel the same way about me? Would that make things better? I don't have time to figure any of that out because it's getting late, and I know Mom is waiting for me outside.

When I get home, I race down to the basement, swing open the door to my girl cave, and open my MacBook. Right away, I get a FaceTime from Mae.

"Oh my goodness, go to your channel right now." Her voice is all business.

When I get to YouTube, I can't believe my eyes.

"Annabelle?" Mae asks.

"Yes."

"Do you see it?"

"Yes."

"Are you dying?"

That's when I let out the loudest "yes" ever. I'm screaming, then Mae starts screaming, then Mom is flying down the stairs to ask what's wrong with me. When she sees me and Mae looking happy, she starts screaming too.

"What are we screaming about?" Mom starts laughing.

I show her my video, which she still hasn't seen.

The guys from DudePerfect shared my video with the comment, "THIS IS PERFECT!"

And now it has gone from 98 views to 453 views in not even a couple of hours! It's been shared 17 times, and I have 28 subscribers. As in actual people who want to see more of my videos.

"Hi, Mrs. Louis." Mae waves from the computer. "Do you see our popular girl, Daphne?"

"Mae, I love it!" Mom says. "And the comments are great. I'm going to call Dr. Varma right now and share the good news."

Mom calls her on speakerphone. "Dr. Varma," she says when the doctor picks up. "Annabelle, Mae, and me here. Have you heard the news?"

"Yes, I see Annabelle's video is doing very well!" Dr. Varma says. "Annabelle, I thought you were going to keep it private?"

Mae chimes in, "I say you keep this going. A share from DudePerfect is, well, perfect. Just look at the views now!"

Not even five minutes have gone by, and I'm up to 506 views, 21 shares, and 30 subscribers.

And there's a new comment: "Are there more videos on this channel?"

I'm nervous but excited. Does that make sense?

Dr. Varma says, "Why don't you think on it a bit if you want to close public access? It's better if this decision is all your own."

I tell everyone I have to sleep on all of this. My fingers itch to do what I do best—make myself invisible and click private. But something inside me says, "Keep going."

12

DAPHNE ON THE RISE

1,203 views. 43 shares. 52 subscribers. This. Is. WILD! And what's even crazier are the comments:

> **SportBarbie**: DudePerfect sent me here. This is HILARIOUS!

> **Sebas125**: The only sport I like is sleeping.

> **DynoMight**: I need more videos. We hate the same stuff.

> **ThunderDownUnder1**: Do another video and make it about school lunch!

> **MaeFromTheUK**: That's my girl, "Daphne!"

These people actually want to see more of ME? I mean Daphne! I think that "private" button might have to wait. Eeep!

13

BREAKING THE RULES

"I see you took matters in your own hands and didn't name the vlog *Daphne Does It All*. You're a take-charge kind of girl," Dr. Varma says.

"Thank you . . . I think?"

"And you have yet to make it private?" she asks.

"I'm up to 1,203 views, and that's just for the sports video. I posted a quick school lunch video right before I came here, and it's already gotten 736 views. Every time I tell myself to click private, something stops me."

"And tell me, is anything different at school? Is it still this awful place that you want to drop out of?"

"Well, not exactly. I met a few people. Like Rachael. She's really popular, but she barely knows I exist. And then there's John—he's funny. And Clairna and Navdeep are pretty cool too. I eat lunch with them."

"It sounds like you're finding your way at McManus."

I guess I am. It's only been two weeks. I've made three friends. Got in trouble once. But Mrs. Gironda got over it and gave my phone back.

"I was thinking about something. The videos are great, but I'm not convinced you fully accomplished the goal," Dr. Varma says.

"What do you mean?"

"Your videos are becoming a hit," Dr. Varma says. "But I was thinking that we should find something you *do* like to do. Any ideas on what the next topic could be?"

I'm clueless, but it doesn't matter because Dr. Varma is already pulling up the McManus webpage on her tablet.

I can already tell where this is going.

"I think I found the perfect activity for you, Annabelle!"

Note to self: must find a way to hack McManus's website and prevent doctor access.

Dr. Varma moves to my couch so we can see it together.

And there it is:

Audition for the Drama Department's Fall Play:
Little Shop of Horrors!
Monday, October 1 at 3:30 p.m.
No need to have anything prepared. Come as you are!

Dr. Varma flips one arm to her side and does spirit fingers. "Didn't you say this was your favorite movie? Oh this will be *perfect*! I can see it now: 'Daphne Does Drama.'"

How about . . . Daphne definitely does NOT?

14

SAME NIGHTMARE

Being famous isn't easy. I ride up to the entrance of McManus Middle School in my limo. Beyoncé's "Run the World (Girls)" is blasting through the speakers. Crowds are gathered around my limo, cameras out, ready to take selfies with me—star of the newest hit YouTube vlog, *Daphne Doesn't*. I apply an extra coat of Bubble Gum Smash lip gloss and run a brush through my long, straight hair. My chauffeur, also known as Dad, gets out of the driver's seat, comes around, and opens my door. And the fans go WILD! Lights are flashing. Kids are shouting:

"Can I have your autograph, Daphne?"

"You're so cool!"

"Sit at my table at lunch, please?"

"But of course!" I say in my best British accent. The girls are crying. The boys are drooling. And I am loving every. Single. Second.

Clouds begin to move in, blocking the sun. A loud

crack echoes across the sky. The rain comes down in sheets. My perfectly straight hair gets drenched, my trendy, straight-off-the-runway outfit morphs into my typical: shabby chic. Everyone is laughing, snorting, pointing—you know how this goes. Next comes the evil witch laughter sound effect, followed by a piercing scream.

AHHHHH!

My alarm goes off. Dream over. Back to being Annabelle Louis, the Air Force brat from Germany. I jolt upright, see myself in my dresser mirror, and yep, it's still me. Same hair. Same clothes. Same living nightmare.

15

HOT STUFF

Welcome to the never-ending comedy-horror movie that is my life.

Here I am dragging myself to tryouts after school for *Little Shop of Horrors*. The title is fitting—middle school really is a place of horror.

When I get to the auditorium, the drama director, Mr. Davis, is passing out scripts. I take one and go *wayyyy* in the back of the auditorium to sit—the very last row. In theory, this all sounds easy. Read a few lines. Do a couple of simple dances. Sing a tune.

John finds me in the back of the auditorium and rushes my way. Sometimes I wonder if he has sniff detectors the way he always seems to find me. "What happened to the cow who auditioned for the play?" he asks.

"I don't know."

"He got *mooed* off stage." John laughs, and I can't help but do the same.

Mr. Davis rings a bell to get everyone's attention. "Ladies and gentlemen, please take a seat in the first couple of rows. We are about to get started with our auditions!"

I let out a sigh and trail behind John to the front. And by trail, I mean shoulders caved, feet slow-dragging against the floor, praying no one is looking at me. Meanwhile John is skipping and snapping down the aisle, to which Mr. Davis cheerfully says, "That's the spirit!"

He calls the boys up to the stage first. He reviews some "simple" dance moves. Four grapevines, four turn-claps, and for the finishing touch, a fist-pump leap toward the sky. *Easy enough,* I think. Then he reviews a short verse of "Suddenly Seymour" and has all the boys sing along. Next, he calls up the girls to do the same.

You might think this part is easy because there's a group of us, all braving the stage together. But did I mention how much I LOATHE doing anything in a group? This is starting to feel like Sports Day all over again!

I tuck myself in the back line and move through the dance steps. My brain tells my feet and legs what to do, but it appears that all of my limbs are on strike today. The other students move together in sync. And there I am crashing into girls left and right.

One of those girls happens to be Rachael, who's in the row in front of me.

The first time I bump into her, she doesn't say anything. Just turns around and gives me a look mad enough to melt my face off. It's the third kick in her ankles that sends hot fire spewing from her mouth: "I hope you don't call this dancing! You need to get your whole life together, girl!"

It feels like someone punches me in the gut. Hard. Somebody, anybody, get me out of here!

The girls around us start laughing. I stop "dancing." Clairna gives me a reassuring look. Finally, I catch up on the last three counts, in time to hit the last pose.

Thankfully, Mr. Davis calls us all back to our seats. But then he announces he'll be calling us up in twos to read lines from the script.

First up is John, who's paired with Rachael. The whole time they read their lines, my eyes are glued to John. He nails it. John is a living, breathing Seymour Krelborn! From the scruffy hair to the wire-framed glasses, right down to his penny loafers!

The music begins. Rachael and John begin to sing and dance. Rachael's dancing flawlessly. She doesn't miss one step. John tries to keep up with her, always moving half a beat behind her, but for some strange reason, it works. And they sound great together, singing. Usually John doesn't get much attention, but when their scene is over, everyone claps really loud.

"John, your voice is as lovely as your trumpet playing!" Mr. Davis says.

"I'm what they call a triple threat," John responds, and takes a bow.

Mr. Davis calls up the next group. After John and Rachael's performance, I'm almost certain it's time to leave. So while the kids on stage perform, I grab my knapsack and start tiptoeing toward the exit.

But they finish quicker than expected. Everyone claps, and Mr. Davis says: "Next up, Annabelle Louis and Austin Coleman."

Busted. Again.

Everyone turns to look at me. My shoulders slump into a pile of mush. I pull the folded script out of my pocket, place my knapsack on a chair, and make my way to the stage. I can feel the entire world staring at me.

Austin is already standing on stage by the time my legs finally decide to get there. I should probably mention that Austin Coleman is music-video, basketball-dribbling cute.

Mr. Davis starts the music. I take a deep breath and try my best to pretend I'm Daphne. Minus the cameras and the cool British accent. *I can do this, I can do this*, I tell myself.

But four counts in, I'm already having a hard time keeping up with Austin—who, might I add, is now officially dance-star cute. He goes left, I go right. Not one move is coordinated, and I can't find a way to control my spaghetti arms and legs, even though my mind is screaming at my body to do what Austin is doing. How can dancing be this hard?

He sings the first line of "Suddenly Seymour," and when I join him, in harmony, things start to seem better. No one is laughing, so that's good. I'm coasting through the lower notes, voice smooth as a baby's bottom. I start to really get into it too. Close my eyes. Picture myself singing in front of millions of screaming fans. Hello, Daphne, and goodbye, Annabelle! But then I go for the high note. It comes out in the key of squeal.

And cue theme music to Jaws!

My voice cracks, and somehow the note I was supposed to hit morphs into something like a call to the wild.

Eyes open. Mouth drops. Soul is crushed. I could have done much better if I was alone in my girl cave, just me and my camera.

Mr. Davis scrambles to cut off the music.

"Let's move on to the script," he says nervously.

John gives me a thumbs-up from the audience even though I know I just blew it.

Austin and I start to read back and forth, this time no dancing and no singing. By the second line, I don't even need the script anymore. I've seen this show so many times, I could probably recite the lines backward. Thirty more seconds of this horror show, and I'm done.

"Great job, you two!" Mr. Davis says as Austin and I exit the stage, but I know he's lying.

When auditions are over, Mr. Davis leads everyone in a round of applause.

"Everyone was excellent! I'll announce the cast tomorrow, so stay tuned. In the meantime, I'll pass around a list for behind-the-scenes activities, so be sure to add your name if you'd like to volunteer."

By the time I get the list, I notice the lines for stage crew are empty. Maybe I should do that? It's better than embarrassing myself in front of a whole audience. Then at least I can satisfy Dr. Varma's request to participate in extracurricular activities.

For some reason, my inner Daphne voice takes over and says: *There's no way you'd embarrass yourself.* But of course I don't listen. I add my name, pass the list to John, and throw away any thoughts of being in the spotlight. Even if it did feel good for a millisecond when I was singing.

After the way today's auditions turned out, I'm convinced that this drama stuff is not my cup of tea.

16

THE RESULTS

Mr. Davis makes an announcement over the loudspeaker the next morning. "Will everyone who auditioned for *Little Shop of Horrors* report to the auditorium during seventh period? Late passes will be given out. Our meeting will be brief."

I spend the whole day nervous about the play. Meanwhile, by the time I get to my locker at the end of the day, YouTube notifications have blown up my phone. Over three thousand views for "Daphne Definitely Doesn't Do Sports." And 1,500 views for school lunch! Wow!

Those kind of numbers will have you thinking that you're hot stuff. Especially when they leave comments like:

"You're so cool, Daphne!"

"Keep the vlogs coming!"

And the best one yet:

"I wish you went to my school."

John catches me looking at my own video for like the fiftieth time. "Someone's obsessed," he says.

There's a yank in my stomach. I turn the screen off and slip my phone into my knapsack. "No, not at all," I say. Then I add, "She's OK, I guess."

"She's hilarious. Actually, I think you kinda look like her." He flashes me a smile so wide that his dimple sinks deep into his cheek.

And then my stomach starts doing this little wave thing again.

"How do you think you did in the audition?" he asks.

"Ha!" I laugh. "I was probably the worst one up on that stage."

John shakes his head. "Nope! I think you're in!"

Just then I see Rachael and company at the popular table, smack in the middle of the cafeteria where everyone can notice her. She must *feel* me staring. And I don't know why I am. But I half-wave, half-smile, like some helpless puppy waiting for my fur-ever family to *Pick me! Pick me!*

For a split second, it looks like she wants to return the smile, rescue me from the entrapment of dorkdom, crown me equally as popular as her. But then, her whole face changes. Like she remembers the number of times I kicked and bumped into her yesterday. That's when she gives me a major eye-roll and returns her attention to those who matter most: her loyal subjects.

The seventh-period bell rings, and we head to the auditorium.

Mr. Fingerlin is in the hallway as we walk by. "Annabelle, you tried out for the play?" He's totally excited. "It's great to see you settling in so fast."

I flash a fake smile and mutter to myself, "Not sure how settled I am just yet."

John asks, "If you're not into drama, why'd you try out?"

I almost say "my therapist," but then I stop myself. Because what if he thinks it's weird that I go to therapy? But saying "my mom made me do it" would be just as embarrassing, so I just go with, "I wanted to try something new."

At least it's half true.

"What are you into, then? I mean . . . since drama is new to you?"

"Computers. I'm a techie."

"Yes, I remember your first day when I caught your backpack and your MacBook almost fell out."

"And that's why I don't want to bring it anymore," I joke.

Mr. Davis is waiting in the auditorium with tons of boxes on the stage. "Settle down, everyone!" he says. "Come in and take a seat." He pulls out a sheet of paper. "I'm happy to report that everyone did a great job yesterday—all thirty-one of you."

Everyone starts clapping and cheering.

"And because I think that drama is an art form all students should experience, I have decided to include *all* of you in the play."

Everybody jumps up and claps. I stand up too, slowly realizing that holy goodness, I'm in a play. And suddenly, I don't know how to feel. Happy? "Lit"? Scared? Or all of the above?

D. Final answer.

John leans over and says, "Told you Mr. Davis was cool like that!"

"OK, take a seat. Now, running a dramatic production isn't only about acting on a stage. There's choreography, set design, lighting, music, understudies, tickets, and so much more. That said, some of you will do double duty. Some will be more behind the scenes, which is just as important. And with the play premiering on Halloween, we'll need to get to work right away! Are we ready to find out who our cast is for *Little Shop of Horrors*?"

We all start shouting again. And I don't know why,

but I realize I want to hear my name called. I want it so badly, I stop breathing as Mr. Davis talks.

He begins by announcing the production crew: "Running sound, music, and lighting will be Ruby Valentin, Matthew Davis, and Navdeep Singh."

Navdeep turns to me, John, and Clairna and slaps us all high fives.

Still not breathing.

"For set design, we have . . . Nicholas Rocco . . . Clairna Joseph . . .

Suffocating in five, four, three . . .

"and Annabelle Louis."

Clairna yelps and gives me a hug. I, Annabelle Louis, will design the set for *Little Shop of Horrors*! Mom and Dad are going to lose their minds!

Then Mr. Davis moves on to announce the acting roles. The roles of Crystal, Ronette, and Chiffon go to three of Rachael's friends, loyal subjects numbers one, two, and three. Mr. Mushnik will be played by Raheem Hannibal, and Bryan Tucker will play Orin, the dentist.

"Playing the lead of Seymour Krelborn is Johnathan Lopez!"

John squeezes my hand so hard I think he'll crush my bones.

"And the understudy for Seymour will be Navdeep Singh!"

Navdeep and John bump fists.

"And finally for our female lead, Audrey."

Everyone gets really quiet as the tension builds, even though we already know who it is. . . .

"Rachael Myers!" Mr. Davis yells, and the crowd goes wild. "And the understudy for the role of Audrey . . . goes to Annabelle Louis!"

I'm sorry. What did he just say?

Silence. Then one clap (from John). Then another (Navdeep) and another (Clairna). And a few more claps, followed by whispers of: "Oh, that's the girl from Germany!"

Someone hand me a spatula to scoop my mouth off the floor! Did Mr. Davis really just choose me to be an understudy? For Audrey? I was awful yesterday!

Rachael turns around and says, "Congrats." But there's that eye-roll thing again.

I'm trying to stop the tears from welling up. I'm happy for Rachael (even with her rolling eyes), and scared for me, but can I also say, happy for me too?

That's when I realize that I'd been lying to myself. That I don't do drama. That I don't like it . . . or sports . . . or anything, really, that involves school. But here I am, jumping up and down in my seat, happy, and not fake-happy, but real, live, I'm-going-to-be-in-a-play happy!

Could it be that maybe, just maybe, I'm starting to like this thing called drama?

And cue inner dialogue battle!

Annabelle: NOPE!

Daphne: LIAR!

17

NEW VLOG POST

Mom is already home by the time Dad and I arrive. I told him the news in the car and made him promise to keep his mouth shut so I could be the first to tell Mom.

"How did everything go?" Mom asks as she puts some groceries away.

I feel the heat rising up to my face. I can barely hold it in. "I got not one but two parts! I am going to design the set, and I'm understudy for the lead role."

Mom pulls me in for a squeeze, then we start jumping up and down together. Then she stops and pulls me back to take a look at me.

"Hmm . . . I thought you didn't do drama!" Mom says sarcastically.

"I'm just an understudy. I won't have to be on stage, at least, in front of all those people. Rachael will make sure she's in the spotlight no matter what."

Dad searches the cabinets for a pot, and I'm already

drooling, thinking of what he'll make for dinner tonight.

"Speaking of people, have you seen the views now? Over five thousand and counting for sports and almost four thousand for school lunch! It doesn't look like it's slowing down. People want to know when you'll post your next video," Dad says.

A tiny part of me wonders what would've happened if I'd done better yesterday. Would *I* have gotten the lead role? How can I vlog about something I wanted to hate, but actually ended up sort of liking? And there goes my movie-making brain, with a voiceover that says: *Time for a re-take.* I feel a new vlog coming, and this time it'll be just what the doctor ordered. But first . . . homework.

* * *

Boy was I wrong about Dad making dinner. Just when I was craving pasta Bolognese and garlic bread, Mom dashed my hopes and gave Dad a break.

Tonight's specialty? Hot dogs and beans. Yuck! Dad and I sit through dinner pretending like it was the best meal we've ever had. I am starting to get good at this acting thing!

After dinner, I help Dad wash the dishes and then I steal away to my girl cave. The role of Audrey is calling me. This is my chance for a do-over—a chance to show what I would have done if I'd had my equipment with me. I sift through the racks of clothes and find *the* most perfect outfit for *Little Shop of Horrors*: a vintage-looking cream-colored dress with red roses and a short blond wig with baby-pink highlights. One coat of bright-red lipstick, and I am transformed into Audrey.

And lights, camera, action!

"Hi, guys! It's your girl, Daphne. And I have a confession. My first video was called 'Daphne Definitely Doesn't Do Sports,' and in that video I talked about the top five reasons I think sports are simply dreadful. Because this channel is a social experiment, I was supposed to try new things that I might discover I like . . . such as sports. But we all know that was an epic fail. So yeah, I broke the rules. Sorry, Mum. But today I'll play nice and do what I was supposed to do all along. Today's episode is . . ."

And cue drumroll . . .

"'Daphne Does Drama'! So, it's no secret that I love movies. I make them, I dream of them, and sometimes when I'm feeling really creative, I'll act out a scene— even if it's mostly in my head. But it just so happens that I love *Little Shop of Horrors*! I mean, who doesn't? Set in the 1960s. A bloodthirsty plant that snacks on humans to survive. There's singing, dancing, a budding romance. Pure perfection! So, ladies and gentlemen, playing the LEAD role of Audrey—it's *moi*, Daphne."

Insert loud applause.

I blow kisses to my imaginary adoring fans. "Oh, you guys are far too kind!"

I do away with my British accent and change my voice to make it squeaky like Audrey's. "This will be a reading of my favorite lines in the play." I take a deep breath, then begin my monologue: "I dream of a place where we could be together at last . . ."

When I'm done I take another bow, and the applause track plays again. Editing everything is super easy. I drop the clips in iMovie and throw in some cool transition tricks.

Just then Mae sends me a text with a picture of herself. Surprisingly, she's dressed in a wig and an over-the-top outfit.

> **Mae**: You're going to be so popular, girl, I'm dressing up as Daphne for Halloween!

Still dressed in my costume, I head to the bathroom upstairs while typing a text back.

> **Me**: Mae, there's no Halloween in the UK.

> **Mae**: Well, there will be after this. Just check your views, *amiga*!

I click on my YouTube channel, and oh my stars, my two vlogs now have a combined total of . . . 11,200 views!

I send Mae another text.

> **Me**: Just uploaded a third video a few minutes ago. Take a look and let me know what you think.

I take my wig off, and it drops to the floor. But I'm way too tired to pick it up.

I send Mae a pic, holding up two fingers, for two *amigas*. She sends back a picture of herself doing the same.

Just like the script from *Little Shop of Horrors* says, *I dream of a place . . .*

I add my own words to that line . . . *a place where Mae and I could be together again.*

18

WANNABE

Mr. Davis wastes no time preparing us for the play. There's practice after school Monday through Thursday, two hours each day. Things are super busy these days, and I am finally starting to feel like I have a social life. Not to mention balancing homework and my vlog.

During rehearsal the past two days, Nicholas, Clairna, and I have assembled the stairs for the pet shop scene, colored in the floor tile paper, and painted the Little Shop of Horrors sign, complete with blood dripping from the letters. Today's project: tackling that overgrown, man-eating plant, Audrey II.

Mr. Davis runs lines with John and Rachael at center stage, while Mrs. Gironda reviews choreography with the rest of the cast. Even though we've only been practicing for two days, we're running like a well-oiled machine!

"Navdeep, Annabelle, stop what you're doing and run this same part." Mr. Davis has John and Rachael take a seat in the front row. This has been the norm. The actors rehearse their parts, and then Mr. Davis calls in the understudies to do the same.

Nav and I take our place at center stage. Nav holds the script, hands shaking, and looks at me with wide eyes.

"In three, two, one, action!" Mr. Davis yells out.

Nav begins reading from the script. When it's my turn to speak, I let the words flow naturally, picturing myself as Daphne, the fearless YouTuber.

When I finish my last line, Mr. Davis calls, "Cut!"

Everyone claps, and Nav and I take a bow.

"Excellent work! Annabelle, you already have the script memorized?" Mr. Davis asks.

"Yes, sir." I shift my eyes to Rachael and try to gauge the meaning of the look on her face.

Mr. Davis sends Nav back to the sound booth and me back onstage to help Clairna and Nicholas finish building Audrey II, the flesh-eating plant.

"Dude, that was amazing!" Nicholas says. "You could have totally played the lead role."

"Yeah!" Clairna chimes in.

"I don't know. I love what we're doing." The words feel stale coming out of my mouth. "This is more exciting, the behind-the-scenes stuff."

Do I really mean that, though? Because performing

that scene for my vlog last night felt pretty darn amazing. Still, building the set is right up my alley. It's like re-creating my girl cave all over again, only on a bigger scale.

It's OK to like both, right? To secretly like the spotlight *and* create stage art with my hands?

And cue inner dialogue battle again!

Daphne: Of course it is!

Annabelle: Nope. Pick a team!

Clairna pulls out the green paint so we can color the large head of the plant. Just then someone's phone beeps. We all pause to listen if it's our phone.

"Whoops, that's me!" Nicholas pulls his iPhone out of his back pocket, swipes the screen, and his whole face lights up.

"What is it?" Clairna asks.

"That's weird," Nicholas begins. "Here we are running rehearsals for *Little Shop of Horrors*, and a video of that Daphne girl pops up and guess what she's performing?"

Clairna yanks the phone out of Nicholas's hand. "No way!"

I breathe in deep and then move next to Clairna to see.

"I'm telling you, sometimes I think the Internet is like, stalking our lives," Nicholas says.

Clairna clicks the play button, and we all watch together. There I am on the screen playing the role of Audrey, and here I am in real life dying faster by the second.

"Eh, I don't know about this one," Nicholas says. "Her sports video was a LOT funnier."

And cue speed-racing heartbeat!

Clairna throws in an extra blow. "Agreed. The lunch one too. This one's all serious and stuff."

Before I get a chance to throw in my bit—*well, I think this is pretty good, considering I'm the human version of a turtle!*—Mr. Davis catches us slacking off. He leaves John and Rachael and joins us near the overgrown plant. "Guys, we're supposed to be building a set, not playing on our phones."

"Sorry, Mr. Davis," Clairna says sincerely. "It's just—there's this YouTuber who posted a video of herself performing a monologue from *Little Shop of Horrors*."

"Yeah, *ummm*, we *ummm*, wanted to show you how amazing it is!" Nicholas says.

Nicholas hands Mr. Davis the phone, and he presses play. Right away, Mr. Davis starts wrinkling his nose and twisting up his face.

That's when I know for sure my video stinks worse than Limburger cheese. (I love my German food, but that one's got to go!) It's not only his face that says it, it's the number of views: A whopping six! No comments? No shares?

And I posted it almost 24 hours ago! Mr. Davis watches to the end and then marches backstage with Nicholas' phone still in his hand.

"What is he doing?" I ask.

"Looks like somebody got jacked for his phone!" Clairna teases.

"Not funny, Clairna! I just got that for my birthday." Nicholas crosses his arms like a toddler.

Mr. Davis returns with a television on a cart with wheels, rolls it to center stage, and connects Nicholas' phone to the screen.

This isn't happening.

He clangs the bell, making everyone stop what they're doing. "Everyone gather around," he says. "Take a seat in the first few rows."

This can't be happening.

The cast and crew fly to the seats. John beckons for me to sit next to him, which also happens to be beside Rachael.

"It seems that our set designers have found a lovely video of an actress performing a scene from our play. And I wanted to share it with you."

I whisper to no one in particular, "I didn't find anything! Leave me out of it!"

As soon as he presses play, every single body part of mine loses functionality. Any second now, I'm going to vomit. In three . . . two . . .

The video ends right before I spontaneously combust.

Everyone starts clapping. I feel Rachael's eyes on me. This is it. *She knows.*

I shift my gaze on her. Rachael whispers, "I've never even heard of that girl." The five-hundred-pound weight on my shoulders poofs away.

"This, dear cast, is commitment!" Mr. Davis is all riled up. "The characterization, the accent, it's flawless! We can all learn from this."

Mr. Davis seems to look at Rachael, and she sinks into the chair.

Meanwhile I look around at kids and hear them whisper:

"What's the name of that YouTuber?"

"Oh, the I-hate-sports girl?"

"I liked the school lunches video better."

"OK, enough of the chit-chat, guys!" Mrs. Gironda, chief cell phone snatcher, yells out. "We have to finish up rehearsals."

"Yes, now run along! Back to work!" Mr. Davis shoos everyone off to their various locations in the auditorium.

John leans in to Rachael and me. "That was really

good. She kind of reminded me of you, Annabelle. Right, Rachael?"

Before I can even answer, Rachael says, "I'm not going to take pointers from some *wannabe* YouTube star! You know what I'm saying?"

She looks straight at me.

On the inside, I feel myself breaking, piece by piece. That wannabe is me.

But I just nod, because I *think* that's what you do when the most popular girl in school offers you a breadcrumb of attention. Then I say, "You got that right, girl!"

19

DAPHNE DOES DRAMA

Nine views. Zero shares. Zero new subscribers.

I didn't think it could get much sadder than this. But then I saw the comment. Yup. Not plural. Just one:

TooCoolForSchool: Go back to your Daphne Doesn't format. Quick!

Point taken!

20

GROUP PROJECT

The next day Mr. Davis starts off history class with a special announcement. "This week we will focus on the Age of Exploration." He paces up and down the rows of seats. "Now, who can name some famous explorers?"

Nicholas raises his hand. "Ooh, Christopher Columbus!"

"Aka civilization destroyer," John blurts out, and the whole class laughs. John straightens his shoulders like he's proud of himself.

"There is truth to that, John," Mr. Davis says. "Christopher Columbus' expeditions ushered in a movement that began the transatlantic slave trade and wiped out millions of indigenous people."

I don't want to speak, I try not to speak, but ACK! This was Mae's and my favorite history topic, and I just have to say something! "Columbus wasn't the only one, though. There were other people before and after him."

The whole class is staring at me. Mr. Davis stops walking and leans back a bit. "Do tell, Miss Louis."

Oh dear. Here come the eyeballs. Lots of them. And they're all pointed at me. I clear my throat and try to block them out. "Well, there were several European countries that wanted to find new trading routes so they could discover new lands, silks, and spices. So people like Amerigo Vespucci and Marco Polo were responsible for enhanced methods of navigation and mapping, which sort of turned geography into science, and—"

"This ain't science class, girl!" Rachael says a little too loudly.

And cue laughter and not-so-whispery whispers!

"Annabelle is a real nerd."

"How does she know all that stuff?"

"Because she's not from this planet."

That last comment sends a cold shiver down my back.

"Settle down, everyone." Mr. Davis claps three times. "What a nice tie-in to this week's assignment, Annabelle!"

As soon as Mr. Davis turns his back and walks to the front of the room, John holds out his fist for me to pound it. Then Mr. Davis says two fatal words that remind me of reason number 391 why I never liked going to regular school: "group projects."

Note to self: Here's your next vlog! "Daphne Definitely Doesn't Do Group Projects."

For the two and a half years I went to school in Spain, I would get stuck doing all the work. Every. Single. Time. By the time we moved to the UK, I was over it.

"OK, class, stand up and step away from your chairs," Mr. Davis orders. "Now, because I like to make things as democratic as possible, I'm going to give you exactly thirty seconds to create a group of three. In four . . . three . . ."

I can feel John's eyes piercing my skull, but he's not the only one.

"Two . . . one!"

John dashes to my side, and Rachael does a ballerina leap over her seat, knocking it over to join him. Two seconds ago she was making fun of me. And now here she is, clinging to my side like we're *amigas*.

Other kids are bum-rushing their way to get to our group.

"Don't even think about it!" Rachael warns.

A few sighs, followed by random mumbling. "Oh man, I wanted to be in Annabelle's group!"

The thirty-second time limit ends, and there are still a few stragglers walking around with disappointed faces. That doesn't stop Mr. Davis from reminding them they have no choice but to team up and make it work.

"Excellent!" he says once everyone has found a group. "Now, every group will pick out of a hat. Your card will have the name of the explorer you will research. You'll have a week to pull together your project. For the presentation, I'll let you decide how you will share your information. Act, sing, dance, make a Prezi—whatever you can creatively come up with."

Rachael picks out of the hat for us. "Amerigo Vest . . . poo . . ." she has a hard time getting the name out.

"Vespucci," I finish for her. "America's actually named after him."

Mr. Davis smiles. "You really know your history, Annabelle."

On the inside, I'm whispering, "Thank you, Mr. Tanaka." Mae's dad is the biggest history buff I know.

"Guys, we're gonna need to set up some time after school to get this done," John says.

He's right. Between other homework, play rehearsals, and making Daphne videos, I'm definitely going to need some outside time to work on this.

"Good idea, but where?" Rachael asks. "Umm, we can't meet at my house because . . ."

"My house works!" The words come out so fast, they surprise me.

John shrugs and gives a nod. "Fine by me. When?"

"Let's shoot for tomorrow, after play practice," I say.

"OK, cool," Rachael says.

The bell rings, the classroom empties, and just like that it hits me: tomorrow the most popular girl at McManus will hang out . . . with *me* . . . at my house.

21
CURRY AND CONVERSATION

Tonight's dinner scene is brought to you by spicy food and a spicy mood.

Going live in four, three, two, one . . .

ME
I have some friends coming over tomorrow after play practice. Can you pick us up at 4:30?

MOM
Oooh, *friends*—I like the sound of that! Dr. Varma will too. Which reminds me, I need to make another appointment soo—

DAD
(*cuts Mom off*)
Who exactly are these *friends*?
(*loosens tie around neck*)

ME
Rachael Myers and Johnathan Lopez. We have a social
studies project to work on.

MOM
Ah, history was my favorite in middle school. What
topic?

ME
European Age of Exploration. We're researching
Amerigo Vespucci.

DAD
(*complexion deepens two shades*)
Is he ugly?

ME
Dad, all of those ancient explorer guys were
weird-looking, if you ask me.

Cue theme music for the movie Jaws.

DAD
(*half-choking on a chicken bone*)
The boy. Is the boy ugly?

*Zoom in on Mom laughing, me grabbing water to mellow out
Dad's famous curry chicken.*

ME
Um, no. Wait, I don't know. Maybe. What kind of
question is that?
(*morphs slowly into a glob*)

MOM
Aww, I think Annabelle has a little *novio*, Ruben.

ME
Don't do that, Mom. He's not my boyfriend.

DAD
(*transforms into a human habanero pepper*)
I'll pick you up from school, but I need parent phone numbers. You can work in the living room. But he'd better be ugly.

End scene!

* * *

For the record, Johnathan Lopez is not ugly. He's . . . *OK* . . . I guess.

UGH!

22

A CONNECTION

When play practice is over, John, Rachael, and I walk out of the building just as Dad is pulling up.

We hop into Dad's black Equinox, and I'm praying he doesn't say or do anything to embarrass me. "Dad, this is John. John, my dad," I say.

"Hello, Mr. Louis." Johnathan gives Dad a proper greeting, handshake and all.

"Nice to meet you," Dad says. "And good to see you again, Rachael. Buckle up, guys."

Dad turns on the radio, and Rachael immediately says, "Mr. Louis, can you turn it up? This is my song!"

It's the same one with the rapper bragging about his expensive coat. Rachael is singing along and dancing in her seat. And even though I think the lyrics are ridiculous, I start bopping my head up and down like I'm into it too. Dad throws me a smirk, knowing how much we despise this nonsense. But it's almost like he gets it. Like he knows that this is what it takes to make friends.

Minutes later, we get to the house, and I tell Rachael and John to get set up in the dining room. The table is extra long, which will give us plenty of room to spread out our notes.

I walk into the kitchen and find Dad sitting at the breakfast bar, pretending to read the newspaper. But I know better. He keeps peeking out and staring at John.

"Dad, please don't be weird, OK?"

"I thought you were supposed to be meeting friends, like girl friends . . . not *boys*," he whispers.

I laugh and pat Dad on the shoulder. "It's just a school project. Relax."

I pull out a tray from the cabinet to make a quick snack. I line the tray with carrot sticks, hummus, trail mix, and chips. Then I grab a few water bottles from the fridge. As I walk out of the kitchen with my hands full, I notice the door to the basement is wide open. The lighted stairs are screaming, *Come on down!*

"Dad, please don't forget to close the door," I whisper.

"Why?" he asks. "You don't want them to see your awesome girl cave?"

His voice is almost a little too loud. I give him a Rachael-level eye roll. Code for: "I would die!"

Dad gets the message and closes the door as I walk into the dining room.

John and Rachael bum-rush me as soon as I get there. "Snacks!" they scream together.

This is what the next two hours look like: John reciting key points about Amerigo Vespucci's life and expeditions, me taking that information, adding my own notes, and typing it into the Prezi tool on my laptop, and Rachael paying us zero attention.

"Geez, girl." Rachael studies every picture hung on the walls of our living room and dining room. "How many places have you lived?"

"A lot." I keep typing, wondering when she'll actually join us to put in her two cents, but I don't say anything.

John doesn't bite his tongue. "Do you feel like joining in on the fun here, or what?" he asks, taking over my computer to type the next-to-last slide.

"Looks like you guys got it." Rachael brushes John off. "Just make sure you spell my name right. I can't stand it when I'm working in a group and they write my name wrong."

"Funny how you mentioned work, especially when you—"

"I'll just do it," I cut John off, grab the computer, and type all three of our names on the finished product.

Delicious smells from the kitchen begin to travel into the living room.

"What is your dad cooking in there?" John asks.

Nosey Dad, who apparently has been listening all along, yells out, "*Schnitzel*, with a Puerto Rican twist! You guys can stay for dinner if it's OK with your parents."

Please say yes, please say yes!

Just then, Rachael's phone buzzes in her pocket. "Oh shoot! It's already six o'clock. My mom's outside." She looks genuinely disappointed—or maybe I'm imagining it. "I'll take a rain check on that . . . what's it called again?"

"*Schnitzel*. We ate it a lot in Germany. It's like a breaded meat, and Dad makes rice, beans, and plantains to go with it." My stomach gives a roar of approval.

"See you at school, Rachael," John says, "Annabelle, where's the restroom?"

"Down the hall, first door on the right," I say, then I walk Rachael to the porch.

"I saw those pictures of your mom in her Air Force uniform," she says. "My dad's in the military too."

"You never mentioned that before. What branch?" I ask.

Rachael pulls two braids behind her ear. "Army."

"I bet my mom would love to meet him."

"Yeah, that probably won't happen for a while. He's

been deployed for a year. Sometimes it feels like he's never coming home."

I know that feeling all too well, even though Mom's assignments have never lasted more than a couple of weeks.

For the first time, I see something different in Rachael. Not the flashy, diva, non-project-helping, popular Rachael I'm used to seeing at school. This one is open, vulnerable—but that only lasts for a split second. Rachael shakes it off and says, "Whatever. I'll see you tomorrow."

If I'm not mistaken, Rachael and I totally just had "a moment." I might be making another friend at McManus. One who's got adoring fans and who "puts her face on," but one who also just might have some things in common with me. In my mind, I take a picture so I can remember this.

Rachael's mom's car cruises off down Madison Street, and a white minivan pulls up out front immediately after.

"John, I think your ride is—" I can't finish the words because John is already behind me.

Giggling. And holding my wig. Yes, *that* wig. "I found this on the bathroom floor," he says.

Panic takes over. I snatch it from his hands.

"You know, your wig reminds me of that Daphne girl on YouTube."

I laugh a nervous, *get-out-of-here* laugh. "Oh yeah, I never noticed."

"Why do you have that? Got some secret identity I don't know about?" He winks.

I do a quick brain scan for a good lie. "No!" There's my fake laugh again. "It's part of my Halloween costume." My shoulders lower half an inch.

John nods a believing *OK!*

Outside, his *abuela* grows impatient and honks the horn. John grabs his backpack and starts walking down the stairs. Then he stops short and turns around.

"For what it's worth, I think you'd make the perfect Daphne for Halloween."

He throws me a smile, that left dimple sinking in all the way to his skeletal system. And there I am, with my mouth slow-falling toward the steps, watching him walk to the car. John hops in the passenger seat, waves goodbye, and he and his grandmother drive off under a full moon while I stand there wondering, *What the heck just happened?*

23

LAST CALL

Things have been going beyond amazing at school. My grades are good (Mr. Davis gave us an A on the Amerigo Vespucci project). I have some cool friends: John, Clairna, Navdeep. Even Rachael talks to me a little—like in the halls passing by, never at lunch when she's at her diva table. But still, it's something.

And the best part of all is that after a few mix-ups and a couple of paper cuts, the set for *Little Shop of Horrors* is complete. Everyone knows their part. Tomorrow is the day we've all worked these few weeks for: showtime!

Because tomorrow is Halloween, Mr. Davis says that everyone on the stage crew can dress up in a costume of our choice.

Just as our final play rehearsal ends, I get a text.

Dad: Belle, going to be five minutes late.

Me: OK, I'll hang here. Text me when you're outside.

Everyone has gone home, and the auditorium is empty.

"Should I call your parents?" Mr. Davis asks.

I tell him Dad is running late.

"I have to print out the programs for the show," he says. "I'll be in the office. Just pop in and let me know when you're leaving."

"OK," I say.

As soon as the door swings shut behind Mr. Davis, I step onstage and take it all in. The lights, the set that I helped design. Everything is perfect. I don't know what takes over me, but I start reciting my favorite part of the play, just like I did on my vlog, but this time even better.

"I don't believe this!"

I press the remote to make the man-eating plant, Audrey II, move her lips.

"Believe it, baby! I can talk!" Audrey II screams.

"Am I dreaming right now?" I place my hand on my chest, exhale dramatically, and take a bow.

A slow clap rings out from the audience. At first I think it's Mr. Davis, but as the shadowy figure walks down the aisle, I realize it's not.

"By all means, continue acting out *my* part." Rachael crosses her arms tightly.

Horror finds its way to my face. "Sorry, I was just fooling around. I didn't mean to—"

"Steal my shine?"

OUCH!

"Anyway, I forgot my notebook." Rachael places her fist over her mouth and lets out a liquidy-sounding cough.

"Of course, you do the scene better." I die a little more after each word.

"Whatever. I get it." Rachael coughs again. "That's one of my favorite scenes too." She finds her notebook, places it in her backpack, and then starts to walk away.

Everything inside of me is crumbling into dust.

"You know," Rachael says as she turns around, "If you weren't so ... I don't know ... *different*, I'd say judging by the way you just performed, you were the real Daphne."

Different. Translation: dorky.

The imaginary camera pulls in tight to my face. *Hello, sweat beads!*

"Not that I watch that or anything," she says flatly.

"Yeah, me neither," I lie. My shoulders collapse into my chest.

"And girl, I was just kidding."

I shrug. "Yeah, totally."

And end scene!

24

IT'S SHOWTIME!

On the opening night of the show, I get a text.

> **Mae**: Good luck tonight. I wish I could be there, but will be rooting for you from across the pond!

Mom helps me dress up as jazz legend Billie Holiday for Halloween. It's totally different from how I typically dress at school, which according to Rachael is *different,* aka dorky. But tonight Mom transforms me into a celebrity. She pulls my curly hair into a low bun. For once, every strand feels like it's in place. She sprays it with hair spray just to make sure. She gives me one of her dresses to wear. Navy blue velvet with a white flower attached to the lapel. And to top it off, a white flower for my hair.

"You look beautiful," Dad says as I come down the stairs.

We drive to McManus, and when we get there the parking lot is packed. It seems like all of Linden showed up to support us on opening night!

"See you after the show!" I kiss Mom and Dad goodbye.

When I walk backstage, I get stares from Navdeep and John.

"Um, hi, Annabelle!" Nav says, his cheeks growing red.

Then John goes, "This costume's even cooler than the Daphne one!"

Before I respond, they both whip around so fast, as if it was choreographed.

Boys can be so weird sometimes!

After that, a few of the cast members and backstage crew start complimenting me.

"Awesome costume!"

"Who are you dressed up as?"

"Duh, she's that singer lady from the old days!"

"Well, well, well, look who decided to dress normal," Rachael says. She is seated at a lighted table with a mirror, guzzling something from a thermos. Her skin looks damp and a little grayish-green. Not her typical golden brown.

"Are you OK, Rachael?" I ask, walking over to her.

"Just a tickle in my throat." She sighs. "And I wish my parents were in the audience. But, whatever. Work comes first. Always."

Rachael begins to *put her face on,* and I'm sure I see tears building up in her eyes. I lean over and give her a hug. She doesn't hug me back though. In fact, she kind of pushes me away.

"I'll be all right," she says.

Mr. Davis yells for us to take our spots because the show is about to begin!

The character trio of Crystal, Ronette, and Chiffon take their places in front of the closed curtains. The music begins, and they belt out the signature song, "Little Shop of Horrors."

Halfway through the song, the curtains open, revealing the shop in all of its glory. The audience erupts in applause and then settles down as the actors begin their lines.

Rachael, as Audrey, enters stage left, while John, aka Seymour, makes loud noises behind the set. John enters the stage, clumsily tripping over his own feet, causing a roar of laughter from the audience.

The story moves through the lives of Mr. Mushnik, the unhappy owner of a failing flower shop, Seymour, an orphan who's totally crushing on Audrey, and then there's Audrey, an urban girl with suburban dreams.

The discovery of a Venus flytrap–looking plant gives them all the kind of hope they need.

The music cues up for "Somewhere That's Green."

Rachael begins singing, "I know he is the greatest!" The first notes come out in perfect pitch to the beat.

I stand in the wings, mouthing each word she sings.

But then: ". . . still" (*cough*) "Seymour's" (*cough*) "a" (*cough, cough*) "cutie!"

"What's up with Rachael's voice?" Clairna whispers in my ear.

I don't know why, but my nerves take over. And I'm not the one on stage. On the inside, I'm whispering to Rachael, *Take a deep breath! You got this!*

But that doesn't stop her downward spiral until the final note.

The curtains close. Clairna, Nicholas, and I change the set for the next scene. Meanwhile, I hand Rachael a bottle of water and a paper towel to wipe her drenched face. Once the curtains open again for the next-to-last scene of Act 1 (feeding Audrey's wackadoodle boyfriend to the overgrown fly trap), Rachael's face turns paler than her blond wig.

She makes it through once more, coughing after every word. It's during intermission when the chaos begins. Clairna and I close the curtains. Rachael makes a beeline toward the garbage can near the stage exit door. She trips a bit, almost misses it, but gets there just in time to empty out the contents of her stomach.

We all rush to her side.

"Are you sick?" someone asks.

I pat her on the back, helping her get the rest out,

holding my breath to block out the smell. Rachael lifts her colorless, sweaty face and says, "I don't feel so good. Can we just extend intermission another few—"

Rachael starts throwing up all over again.

Mr. Davis is panicking now. "Rachael's family in the audience! Find them, NOW! Annabelle, we need you to take over her part!"

Now I feel like *I'm* the one who's going to throw up!

"Absolutely not!" Rachael pipes up. "I didn't work this hard to let her take my spot!" She wipes her mouth with the sleeve of her dress. "I just need about ten more minutes."

Rachael's grandfather arrives backstage with a bottle of ginger ale and a plastic bag. "Her mom had to work late tonight. I'll take it from here," he tells Mr. Davis.

The next thing I know, Mrs. Gironda is shuffling up to me, waving a black leather bag full of props. "Clairna, quick! Help me get Annabelle changed."

The two of them swish me away from the scene to a room backstage. Mrs. Gironda locks the door.

"What's happening here?" I'm so confused.

Neither of them answer. Mrs. Gironda goes into action mode. She tosses Clairna the Audrey wig and makeup bag and orders her to *put my face on*. Clairna starts piling the stuff on like I'm a cake being frosted. Mrs. Gironda hands me a leotard.

"And when you're done, spray this on your bottom," she says.

I move the bottle closer to my face and notice the name: BUTT SPRAY.

"What in the world is this?" I can't hold in my confusion.

"A theater essential, my dear," Mrs. Gironda says. "It'll keep the leotard in place."

Clairna laughs. "Aka wedgie blocker!"

Everything is moving too fast. Mrs. Gironda attaches a body mic to the collar of my dress, unlocks the door, and starts pushing me toward the stage. I don't even have time to say no. "Whew! Perfect timing!" she says. "Intermission is almost over."

The heavy curtains smack me in the face, leaving a tiny opening. The houselights are still up, and everyone is going back to their seats. I spot Mom and Dad making their way down the aisle. When those curtains finally open, I'm not sure which of us will be the first to have a heart attack.

Clairna and Nicholas roll in a second version of Audrey II, the biggest model we created for the set.

"We're ready to begin the second act. Quiet on set! Places, everyone!" Mr. Davis whispers.

Clairna gives me a fist bump before rushing to the side of the curtains.

Mr. Mushnik, Ronette, and I position ourselves at the phones, ready to receive the thousands of calls that are coming in, all thanks to our main attraction, Audrey II.

My pulse is on high speed, mind scattering to remember the lines.

The music cues up. The stage lights rise. I want to crumble right there in the middle of the stage. Or run away and never come back again. But then I see Mom and Dad. And as soon as they see me, Mom starts slapping Dad on the shoulder.

Code for: "Holy moly, Ruben, get your camera out! Our baby is up there!"

I take a deep breath, and suddenly I don't feel so afraid. In my mind, it's just me up there, pretending to be someone I am not. Just like Daphne.

The phones begin to ring off the hook, and the three of us talk over each other.

"Thank you for calling Mushnik and Son. Your favorite florists of Skid Row!"

And I soar like this right through to the end. Never missing a beat, a note, or a line.

When the play is over, we all line up backstage behind the closed curtains, and I hear the whispers.

"Good job, Annabelle!"

"That was amazing!"

I grow taller with every word. The curtains open, and the crowd goes wild.

One by one, Mr. Davis calls the cast members forward. He announces that Rachael Myers played the role of Audrey for the first act, and saves John and me for last. John reaches out to take my hand and winks at me. My stomach does this flippy-floppy thing as I see the spotlight twinkle in his brown eyes.

As soon as the curtains close, everyone scrambles to find their parents. I don't have to look very far. Mom and Dad are waiting at the foot of the stage with flowers.

Mom elbows me in the side when I get to her, "Well, that was quite the surprise! Nice work, sweetie!"

"Yes, you were a real professional up there." Dad kisses me on the forehead.

"Thank you, Mom, Dad." I lean in to my father's embrace, feeling my whole universe warm up.

"Why don't you grab the rest of your things and we'll meet you at the car? K, *Daph*?" Mom winks at me, and she and Dad make their way toward the exit.

When I turn around, Rachael Myers is standing smack in front of me. Empty barf bag in her hand. Her face a little less green.

"Whoa, you scared me! I thought you went home," I say.

"Did your mom just call you *Daph* . . . as in Daphne?"

"How are you feeling?" I ask Rachael.

"Way to avoid the question, Annabelle." She does her signature arm-cross move, though the barf bag makes her look borderline ridiculous.

I squirm a little but keep my cool. "Oh that? Noooo, my mom said I made her *laugh*!"

"I heard what I heard." Rachael doesn't flinch. Then she eyeballs me up and down. "I begged my grandpa to let me stay and see the rest of the play. Hope you enjoyed your little moment. It wouldn't have happened if I didn't get sick."

She starts coughing, spit flying, germs dancing in the air. I take a step back.

"I hope you feel better, Rachael."

"I'm sure you do," Rachael says. Then she walks away, holding on to that empty barf bag as if her life depended on it.

25

I DON'T DO DRAMA

When I get home, I retreat to my girl cave, because even though I should feel on top of the world right now, I don't. I don't want to talk to Mom or Dad. Or even Mae. She texts me around ten p.m., which means it's three in the morning in the UK, which means she literally waited up all night to ask: "Hey, *amiga*! How was the play?"

And for once, I don't respond. I know, I know. Worst. Friend. Ever.

But I need time to sort through my feelings. I don't understand why Rachael seemed so mad at me. I only did what understudies are supposed to do—to step in when I was needed. At first I thought I would like doing drama, but what I'm seeing is that with drama comes "drama-drama," and that is not for me. Suddenly I feel an itch to make a video.

I look at my clothes rack and pick out an outfit—a royal, Victorian dress. I put on a white wig styled in a bouffant, piled high on my head, and bright-red lipstick. I hold a lace handkerchief in one hand for dramatic effect. I set up my camera and scribble down my scenes. A few runs through my lines, and I'm ready to shoot. Counting down in five, four, three, two . . .

"Hey, guys. It's your girl, Daphne, and I'm back with another episode of *Daphne Doesn't*. Now I know in my last video I was all about 'Daphne Does Drama.' But I changed my mind about one thing. I may like drama, but I definitely don't *do* drama, and here's why:

"Number one: Too much makeup. Like, seriously . . . how is it comfortable to walk around with an entire cake frosted on your face?

"Number two: The bright lights blinding you. It's like: Is the white light coming to get me? Is this how it all ends?

"Number three: Eyeballs. Yup, you heard that right. EYES, people!!! When you're on stage, there are people . . . staring at you. And then your heart starts to beat really fast and your hands start to sweat and you try to do what all the books say: Picture everyone in their underwear. But when you do that, you see your grandma sitting in the front row, and she's got hair on her chest. So you try to unsee that whole travesty, but when you do, it's back to the glowing eyeballs. And the fear starts all over again. Now I know what you're thinking: 'But Daphne, there are eyeballs watching you on these videos.' Touché! But! Right now it's just me in my girl cave, with a single camera. The eyeballs come later—when I'm not around. Whew! I've said a mouthful. But seriously, people: beware the eyeballs.

"Number four: Butt spray. 'What is *that*?' you ask. I'm glad you did. Citizens of YouTube, there is a thing called butt spray, and if you can't already tell by the name, it's an adhesive that you spray . . . on your butt . . . to avoid getting a serious case of the wedgies mid-scene. So here you are walking around in your costume like one big sticky-butt zombie. And if you think that stuff comes off easily in the shower, think again. I still have spray in places I'd rather not mention.

"Number five: And last but not least, I definitely don't do drama because, well, I don't do the *other* kind of drama. The catty fighting over roles. This one is better than that one. It's all just . . . exhausting. It's good to do theater if you want to learn how to be a good actress, but, people of YouTube, don't *become* the drama, if you know what I mean. Want to know why? Because in the end there's enough sun for us all to shine.

"That's all for now! Share, like, comment, subscribe. However you're feeling, just go with it!"

26

DAPHNE CLIMBING

19,079 views. 1,850 shares. 3,714 subscribers.

I present a sample of the comments. . . .

Drumroll, please!

BritishBabe: Loving this funny girl! Just cheeky!

ThespianGoddess: Haters gonna hate. Keep doing your thing.

FamousLamous: Def keep the Daphne Doesn't format. Loved the Group Project vlog, too, but this one is a slam dunk.

MaeFromTheUK: My bestie "Daphne" is going VIRAL! Don't get too famous on me, Jersey girl!

Ladies and gentlemen, I believe we're back on track.

27

MAKING THE DEAL

"I see your videos are really picking up steam," Dr. Varma says as I follow her into her office. "I showed the one you did about group projects to my daughter and we were cracking up. I'm telling you, Daphne will be viral before you know it."

Do I want to go viral? I'm not so sure.

I take a seat on her couch, and we begin our session.

"Tell me about your experience at McManus so far," she says.

"As you know, I've made some friends. John is really cool. Clairna and Navdeep are too. And then there's Rachael. Sometimes I don't think I have a lot in common with her. But then I learned something about her that made me think maybe I do."

"And what was that?"

"Her dad is in the army, like my mom. But he's been deployed."

"Well that certainly is a connection."

"He's been gone a year. And I'm starting to wonder if that has anything to do with the way she acts."

"How so?"

"One minute she's half-nice to me. She even came to my house, and she and John and I worked on a presentation together. Well, more like John and I did the work, and she sort of slacked off. But we still got an A on the project, so I guess it all worked out. But then she totally got mad at me over the play, even though she's the one who got sick and couldn't finish her part. I was just doing what I was supposed to do . . . fill in!"

"What do you feel is the source of her wishy-washy behavior?"

"I think maybe it's because she's missing her dad." I get really quiet after that. There's a ball slowly growing in my throat. Am I about to cry? Over Rachael's dad? Or is this about something more personal?

"Will the same thing happen to me . . . when Mom leaves?" I ask.

Dr. Varma leans forward and touches my hand. "We all react differently when it comes to being away from our parents. I think it's good you acknowledge what Rachael is going through. It's probably an even better reason to connect with her. She might benefit from being around someone who understands. Have you told her about your mum's TDY?"

"No, I'm actually trying not to think about it," I say.

"Well, it is November," Dr. Varma says. "The holidays will come fast, Annabelle. I'd say it's time for you to let your friends know. Along with your father, they will be your greatest support system. Also, you have me. I'll still be around." She pauses. "How are you holding up on the Daphne end?"

"I'm starting to feel like it's hard to keep it a secret. I almost got caught a couple of times."

Dr. Varma's eyes widen. "Tell me about it."

I tell her about how John asked to use the restroom at our house and found one of my Daphne wigs in there. And then how after the play, Rachael heard Mom call me Daph, even though I denied it.

"Well that was a close one, wasn't it?"

I nod.

"You know, I have seen you blossom since you first started coming here."

"You have?"

"Oh, yes. You walk with a little more pride in your step. You're certainly less shy. And look, you even have some new friends. And even though things seem strained with Rachael, I think you might have a chance at a real connection with that one."

I smile. It's not like I want to be best friends with Rachael or anything. My best friend is Mae, and even though she's miles away, that will never change.

"So since you already discovered that you don't like sports and you do like drama, but you definitely don't like drama-drama. Let's figure out something else you can vlog about that you might enjoy. Maybe you can tell me what you're thinking."

"Well on the night of the play I dressed up nicely for once. And I don't mean like the over-the-top outfits I wear for my vlog, I mean like a real dress with my hair styled in a way that didn't make me look like a human oak tree. And for that one night I felt, I don't know . . . noticed. But in a good way. Even Rachael said I looked nice. And that girl is like the QUEEN of fashion at McManus."

I can see the light bulb switch on over Dr. Varma's head. "So what you're telling me is you might want to consider changing your wardrobe?"

"Yes. Well, no. Ugh!" My body deflates, and I become one with the couch. "Here's the thing—I like the way I dress. But I also liked the attention I got at the play. It was nice to not be so dorky for a change."

"Define dork," Dr. Varma says.

I run my fingers from the top of my head to the bottom of my shoes, indicating the definition is me.

Dr. Varma smiles. "There's nothing wrong with being a dork. Some of the brightest people call themselves dorks. But I do understand liking the feeling you had when you dressed up. So let's say we title your next vlog as 'Daphne Does Fashion.' It has a nice ring to it, doesn't it?"

I think about that for a moment. And then my internal movie starts up. My perfectly styled hair is blowing in the gentle wind. I'm wearing high leather boots, a cute pleated skirt, and a blazer. People are clapping as I enter the school building. I'm signing autographs and saying words like "darling" and "faaaaaabulous." And this time there is no storm or alarm clock to chase the image away.

I want to have a real moment like that. I can totally do this, with my fashionista mom's help.

"I like it, Dr. Varma," I say. "You've got a deal!"

28

MOMMY MAKEOVER

If there are two words that don't usually belong together in a sentence, it's mom and makeover. But when your mom is a Master Sergeant in the Air Force by day and hot enough to be Beyoncé's sister by night, you shut your mouth and take the help. Because some fashion disasters require complete obedience.

Exhibit A—me. Mom wastes no time going into makeover mode after dinner. She barges into my bedroom, hands full of clothes hangers and the biggest smile on her face. "Let's pick out something really cute for school tomorrow," she says.

It's like she's been dreaming of this moment all her life.

Outside of Mom's typical Air Force uniform (which, I admit, is pretty sharp), my mom is a diva. She has flawless ebony skin, straight hair that she styles with ease, and outfits for days worthy of a runway. But that's not me. Typically my wardrobe screams, "I prefer staying home!"

"What in the world am I supposed to do with all of this stuff?" I sigh, rummaging through the mounds of clothes.

It looks like *Seventeen* magazine threw up all over my bed.

"Listen, as far as fashion goes, you can keep it simple, Annabelle. I get it. You like to be comfortable."

"Now you're speaking my language. Comfort is something I know all about!" I admit.

And suddenly, I remember our time overseas, on base in the UK. The days of taking math class in our kitchen with Mae and Dad . . . and we all wore pajamas. That was the life! These days, it's a struggle to find anything to wear that doesn't make me look like I've spent the whole day watching Netflix.

Mom lets me try on some of her old jeans. All cute. And surprisingly they all fit even though Mom has curvier features.

"Those look great," Mom says.

I look in the full-length mirror hanging on my closet door. She's right. I don't look *that* bad. In fact, I'm pretty sure I saw Rachael wearing a similar pair of jeans last week.

I leave those on, and Mom starts showing me her

shirts. "Since you typically mix your prints, let's try something solid for a change."

She hands me a blush-pink blouse, with just a little frill on the sleeve. Very trendy. Very not me. But I put it on anyway. I look in the mirror again and can't believe how different I already look.

"Mom, this whole outfit looks great!" I say. "It's not even itchy!"

"See? Stylish and comfortable! But there's nothing wrong with dressing casually either. You look beautiful no matter what."

My heart fills and sinks just the same. I know she means it, but sometimes I wonder if she says things like that because that's what moms are supposed to say.

"My hair." I sigh and sit in front of my dresser mirror.

Mom starts playing with a big chunk of it. "What's wrong with it? I love your hair."

"It's just so poofy. Why can't it be straight, like yours?" I complain.

"Annabelle, my natural hair is curly too. I just use a relaxer because it's easier for my lifestyle. But you know the rules."

"Yeah, yeah, yeah . . . no relaxer before I'm sixteen."

Three years and counting!

Mom smiles. "If you want something temporary, I could—"

"Straighten it? Oh, Mom, PLEASE!" I jump out of my seat and hug her. Next thing I know we collapse on the bed.

"OK, Annabelle. I'll straighten your hair, but don't get used to it. Even heated styling tools can damage your hair. And trust me, I know plenty of girls who would pay to have curls like yours."

Mom washes and deep conditions my hair in the laundry room sink. After that she sets up my bedroom with her blow dryer, flat iron, jojoba oil, and some spray in a bottle.

"This is heat protectant spray, so your hair doesn't get damaged from the flat iron." Mom demonstrates how to use the flat iron to straighten my curls. Start at the root and follow with a comb to the ends.

It takes her over an hour to transform my hair from a short mop to long, straight hair that reaches the middle of my back.

"I had no idea my hair was this long!" I scream.

"It's called shrinkage. Natural curls shrink hair to make it look much shorter than it really is," Mom says.

When she is done, she applies a soft pink gloss to my lips.

"Something is missing," Mom says.

"What else could I possibly need? This is perfect! I can't wait to go to school tomorrow."

"Stay here. I'll be right back."

Mom comes back with a necklace in her hand. When she puts it on me, I see what she was talking about. It's a silver chain with a navy blue, sparkly heart-shaped gemstone.

"I love this, Mom."

"My mother gave me this necklace when I was about your age. She was getting deployed and wanted me to have it to think of her while she was gone. I was waiting for the right moment to pass this on to you. I could have done it the other times I left, but those assignments were just a couple weeks here and there. Giving you this necklace didn't feel right then. But now that I'll be in Afghanistan for six months, I want you to have it, keep it safe next to your heart, and know that I'm always there."

"I am never, ever taking this necklace off."

And cue tears! Mom's crying. I'm crying.

Dad knocks on my door. "Hey, what are we boo-hooing about?" he asks, pushing the door open.

Mom shows him the necklace.

"I was wondering when you'd give it to her. You look stunning, Annabelle," he says.

"Thanks, Dad."

"It's getting late. You should get some sleep. Put your outfit on a hanger and wrap your hair in this silk scarf so it doesn't get frizzy," Mom says.

They say goodnight and close the door behind them.
I rush to my phone to text Mae a selfie of the new me.

Mae: Excuse me, who is this? THAT is not Annabelle Louis.

Me: I know, ha! It's my new look. You like?

Mae: Like? How about LOVE? Especially that necklace! You're like Annabelle version 2.0.

Me: Thanks, off to bed. Tomorrow starts my next social experiment: "Daphne Does Fashion."

Mae: You got this, *amiga*!

29

THE NEW KID . . . AGAIN

I step into homeroom, and everyone stops talking. Usually Mrs. Rodriguez has to yell at us to hush our mouths, but not today. As I walk to my seat at the back of the room, I hear the whispers.

"Is that Annabelle?"

"She's not wearing weird clothes today."

"No, I think that's a new student."

Part of me is loving the attention, but there is a small part of me that wants to hop a plane and head straight back to Germany.

Rachael turns around and sort of looks me up and down. But then she smiles a little.

My shoulders ease a bit, and I smile back.

"Why are you all dressed up? The play is over," John says.

"Just felt like doing something different," I half-lie.

Confession #1: My therapist and my mom made me do it.

Confession #2: And I kinda like it.

But I don't say that.

John purses his lips like he has more to say, but he doesn't. Instead, he sinks lower in his chair and sticks his nose back in his notebook.

Clairna leans in and whispers, "Look at you, Miss Diva! Don't get too popular on us now." Then she giggles.

I'm wondering if that's the goal here. Am I trying to be popular? Do I even care?

And then that inner voice whispers, *Yes, you do!*

For the rest of my classes, not one of my teachers recognizes me.

"Are you the new kid?"

"Oh, your hair is different!"

Even the school counselor, Mr. Fingerlin, doesn't know who I am at first.

When the lunch bell rings, John, Clairna, and I make our way to the cafeteria. Navdeep is out sick today.

The McManus Café is famous for putting the word "surprise" on the daily lunch menu. Chili dog surprise, pizza surprise, taco surprise. That last one sent me running to the bathroom on my third day of school! So these days I keep it safe with good old peanut butter and jelly. We take a seat at our "reserved" table in the back of the cafeteria. Near the garbage, with an added bonus of spoiled-milk aroma.

Clairna and I do most of the talking while John pushes lettuce around the lunch tray and says nothing.

"Girl, you will never believe who added me on Snapchat over the weekend." Clairna gets all whispery.

"Oooh, spill it!"

"I'll give you some hints. Soccer team, dark mohawk, sits at queen diva's table . . ." Clairna's voice slows down, and her eyes drift to the side.

I turn around to see what she's looking at.

All of a sudden, Rachael gets up from her table in the middle of the cafeteria and starts strutting her stuff toward us. It's like a scene straight out of a fashion show in Milan.

The lights dim, the spotlight is on her. Katy Perry's *Roar* is playing on the loudest decibel. In slow motion, everyone stops eating and stares at Rachael, who is headed my way.

Everything goes back to regular motion as soon as she gets to our table.

"Annabelle, why don't you come sit with us today?" Rachael says.

A glob of peanut butter settles in my throat.

Clairna looks at me and then softly kicks me under the table. And I'm not sure if that kick means "don't you dare" or "you'd better go, girl!" Then she puckers her lips and shoots her eyes straight to Rachael's table. That's when I know exactly why she wants me to go. . . . *Boys.* John, on the other hand, doesn't even look at me. In fact, he's barely said two words to me all day.

"Umm . . . sure, OK," I say nervously. "Let me grab my things."

I toss out my lunch tray and gulp down half a carton of milk. Because there is no way I'm sitting at Rachael's table with peanut-butter mouth. Not when all of her friends and some of the boys from the basketball team are sitting there.

Remember that fashion show strut? Well, it starts up all over again, and this time all eyes are on her . . . and me. Rachael walks like she owns the place. I try to swing my hips—if I had any—but I know I probably look more like a dog being walked on a leash than anything.

"You guys know Annabelle, right?" Rachael says to her groupies when we get to her table.

I wave shyly.

"Oh yeah, your understudy from the play," one of the girls says, laying it on thick with the word *under.*

"Have a seat," Natasha says.

"So, spill it. What's with the new digs?" Rachael wastes no time getting right to business.

Suddenly I feel stupid saying the truth—that the

reason I dressed up is to step out of my comfort zone. Also because my therapist and parents think I need to try new things to make new friends.

"Oh, I just have an early dinner tonight with my parents. . . ." I search my brain for more details to spice up the story, "in the city, with my dad's company. He's an executive . . . at Cisco."

Only one-third of that is true. But the rest sounds fabulous enough.

"Ooh nice!" another girl, Lauren, chimes in. "I love going to the city. So chic."

"Where'd you get the necklace?" Natasha moves in a little too close to me, lifting the necklace with her hand.

"From some fancy jewelry store with Daddy's executive credit card?" Rachael asks.

"It's a family heirloom, apparently. My grandmother was in the army. She gave it to my mom when she got deployed. My mom gave it to me because . . ."

I can't even say the words.

"Oh." Rachael shrugs, but doesn't say anything after that. In fact, she sort of shuts down after that.

Some of kids at the table start doing army salutes and making silly fighting poses. And the ring leader of them all? Dark, mohawk cut. Super broad shoulders. Soccer shirt. Stuffing straws up his nose.

Steven Chu. Aka Clairna's new Snapchat buddy.

I feel Clairna eyeing me from across the cafeteria. She winks and mouths, "That's him!"

The bell rings, and Rachael storms out of the cafeteria.

"You can sit with us tomorrow, if you like," Natasha says, gathering her tray and the one Rachael left behind.

I see Rachael running toward the bathroom on the other side of the cafeteria. Meanwhile, John's eyes are fixed on me and his face is twisted up like he smells something bad.

"Um, yeah, maybe," I say. "Nice chatting with you guys. See you later."

I'm pretty sure John is taking his time throwing away his tray and walking out of the cafeteria because he wants me to catch up to him and say something, but I need to get to Rachael.

When I get to the bathroom, one stall door is closed and I can hear her sniffling.

"You OK in there?"

She flushes the toilet and comes out of the stall. Whatever makeup she had on has been washed away by the tears she tried to hide from me.

"I'm good. You didn't have to follow me in here. I just had something stuck in my eye."

She's a better liar than I am.

"Did I say something wrong when I mentioned the deployment stuff?" I ask. "If so, I'm sorry."

"Oh, it's cool." She shrugs.

"How do you deal?" I ask.

"Deal with what?"

"Everything, I guess. Your dad being deployed."

"You just do. Fill up your time with activities, like hanging out with your friends, going to the movies, shopping. All of that stuff is important too. Besides, why would you care? You have your mom at home with you."

I chew on my bottom lip. "My mom's being sent to Afghanistan. TDY."

It's the first time I've said those words to anyone outside of my circle.

For a second, it looks like Rachael feels sorry for me.

"Well that T for temporary is nothing but a lie." Rachael splashes water on her face. "Anyway, I'm over it." Rachael's voice returns to snob status. Then she whips out her makeup bag and starts *putting her face on* again.

"Why'd you ask me to sit with you at lunch?"

"No reason in particular." Rachael must feel me staring at the way she does her makeup. "Want me to show you a new trend?" she asks.

"Sure," I say.

She pulls out a brown pencil and starts drawing a squiggly line around my eyebrow. Then she fills it in.

"All the style blogs are talking about this." She hands me the pencil so I can draw the other eyebrow. I look in the mirror, carefully drawing it, wondering if I look stylish or plain ridiculous.

Just then a notification sounds off on my phone. I finish up my squiggly brow and hand her back the pencil. When I open the home screen, I see it's a YouTube update. According to their stats, my last video, "Daphne Definitely Doesn't Do Drama," has over thirty-five thousand views and my channel has nine thousand subscribers. Holy cow! My heart starts racing so fast, I drop my phone on the floor.

Rachael quickly reaches down and grabs it, but not before being nosey.

"Hmm . . . I thought you don't watch that vlog."

"I accidentally followed it. Now I get these silly notifications every now and then."

"You know what I found out about that Daphne girl?" Rachael applies a final coat of lip gloss.

"What's that?"

"That she lives here."

Alert! Alert! Somebody call me an ambulance!

"Um, what do you mean?"

"Like here in Jersey!" Rachael pulls out her phone and scrolls to the comment on YouTube from Mae about Daphne being a "Jersey Girl."

"Oh!" I laugh nervously. "But you know, this state is so big."

"How crazy would it be if she lived close to Linden?"

"Totally crazy. Hey, I thought you don't follow her either."

The brown in Rachael's cheeks deepens. "I don't. I just stumbled on that channel after Mr. Davis showed us that stupid video in drama rehearsal. Remember?"

The second bell rings. Just then Clairna and two older kids walk in.

Clairna gives me a wink as she walks to the sink next to where Rachael and I are standing in front of the mirror.

"Hey, speaking of hanging out, I'm going shopping and maybe to the movies with a few friends this weekend," Rachael says. "You should come. I could help you pick out some new clothes."

What did she say? My stomach is doing backflips, but I try to play it cool. I pull a chunk of hair back behind my ears like I see the teens do in rom-com movies.

"Shopping?" My voice is scratchy sounding.

"Bryan will be there." Rachael giggles.

Clairna starts coughing super loud.

Bryan Green. Stats: Sun-kissed skin. Basketball team. Keeps a fresh haircut like he lives in the barbershop. Smells good. Not that I ever stood close enough to tell, but if I did, I bet he'd smell *woodsy*.

"Oh, that's cool. Is Steven Chu going too?" I ask.

And cue Clairna coughing again!

Rachael twists her face at Clairna, but doesn't even ask if she's OK.

"No, I don't think so."

Without Rachael noticing, Clairna presses on my foot, gentle at first, then harder.

"*Oww,* I mean, aww . . . that's fine." I curl my toes inside my Mary Janes. "I think I can fit it in my *sched.*" I shorten the word because I hear the kids doing that all the time around here.

"Here, take my number." Rachael grabs my phone and types in her info. "Saturday. Four o'clock. Aviation Plaza." And then she heads for the exit.

"Bye. Um, see you around there, I mean then. . . ."

The door slams shut.

"I can't believe you're going shopping with Rachael Myers!" Clairna squeals.

"I tried to work you in there with the Steven angle, but—"

"I heard that. . . . ugh!" Clairna's smile fades. "Whatever. Who cares? Annabelle, I think maybe she's starting to finally see what we've seen all along: that you are one cool chick."

30

DAPHNE GOES SHOPPING

Dad has a conniption mid-drive when I tell him that after shopping, the girls and I are going to the movies "with some guys from school."

"Guys?" His neck goes beet red, and he almost loses control of the steering wheel.

"It's not a big deal, Dad."

Mom butts in. "Put a sock in it, Ruben. Our girl's growing up." She turns to me. "You can go, but we'll pick you up right after the movie is over, you hear?"

"Yes, Mom."

Mom and Dad drop me off at Aviation Plaza, right in front of the Kicks USA store. At first I don't see anyone, so I just stand there waiting.

"If you need us we'll be right there in Target," Dad calls out the window. "I have my phone on me . . . and a baseball bat in the trunk."

Mom starts cracking up.

"Please don't be weird and follow me around," I shout back.

"We promise. Have fun with your new *friends*," Mom says. Then they finally drive off.

I shuffle around on the sidewalk and stare at the dried leaves scattering across the pavement. A few minutes later, I get a text.

Rachael: Hey girl, almost there.

It's not long before a car pulls up and Rachael, Natasha, and Lauren step out and wave Mrs. Myers off.

"Ready for some shopping, girls?" Rachael yells.

We all laugh and go inside the Kicks store.

"Having a collection of fresh kicks is essential when you're in middle school," Rachael says to me, like I'm a student in her personal fashion academy.

I walk around taking note of every style she suggests, but on the inside, I'm gagging at the prices. $129 for a pair of sneakers! I could rack up at Trölodei with that kind of money.

"You should try these on." Natasha holds up a pair of Nikes with a sparkly glitter-gold symbol.

Too flashy. Totally not my style, but I just go with it and say, "Sure!"

When I put them on, I still feel the same way, but the girls are *ooh*-ing and *ahh*-ing about how "lit" they are.

"You should get them!" Rachael insists.

I don't tell her that I only have a hundred dollars saved from my allowance.

"I think I'll pass," I say.

"Well if you don't want them, I'm scooping these bad boys up."

Rachael and Natasha grab the same sneakers. I have to get something, so I follow Lauren to the clothing section. She's got her hands full with jeans and tops. I check to make sure no one is watching and head to the clearance rack. I pick up a T-shirt that's on sale for nine dollars.

"That's all you're getting?" Rachael asks when we get to the register.

"Yeah." My cheeks go red. "I'm holding out for the good stuff at the other stores we go to."

"Ah, I see your strategy! You're gonna love Old Navy and Mad Rag."

We pay for our things and then walk out of the store. As we walk, I spot the Second Chance thrift store, where Mom and I went shopping for Daphne outfits. I kid you not, in the store window, I see a shirt similar to one from Kicks that was almost sixty dollars. But here at Second Chance, it's priced at three dollars. THREE DOLLARS!

Oh, I MUST go in! "Guys, let's check this place out," I say aloud.

Rachael, Lauren, and Natasha make faces like they just smelled fresh roadkill.

"I know you're new to the country and all, so let me school you on some things," Rachael says. "This is a hand-me-down store. The clothes in here are not . . . how would you say . . ."

"Um, *lit*! They're clothes for, like, old people!" Lauren chimes in.

But my hand is already on the door and I'm halfway into the store. The girls follow me in, probably to change my mind.

I see so many cool things here, and they're begging for me to buy them. With ninety-one dollars left, I could do some real damage in this store. I snatch a burgundy velvet vintage dress off the rack.

"You're kidding, right?" Rachael eyes the dress skeptically.

Just then, I see the lady from the last time I shopped here with Mom—Georgia. Her eyes light up when she recognizes me. And then I remember how Mom told this sweet lady ALL of my business while we were shopping.

I toss the dress back on the rack like it's garbage. "Totally playing with you guys!" I lie as blue as the sky. "Let's go."

"Oh, I thought so," Natasha says.

"Yeah, let's get out of here!" Lauren says.

But Georgia's already moving in on us. "Hey! I remember you!"

The girls give me weird looks. But I keep pushing us along.

That doesn't stop Georgia from following us. "How'd everything go with that show you were working on?" she asks.

Rachael looks at me, confused.

"Oh, the play?" I say. "Yeah, that was fun. Big turnout. Nice seeing you, gotta go!"

I'm really pushing the girls out now, moving farther and farther away from Georgia.

"But I thought it was something with the computer?" she mumbles, and I pray I'm the only one who heard her.

"What was all that about?" Rachael asks.

We cross the parking lot and head to Old Navy. I see Mom and Dad walking into Marshalls, but they don't see me. Thank goodness!

"Um, not really sure. Probably a bad memory!" I say.

"Yeah, old people!" Rachael says.

All the girls start laughing.

I decide I can't afford another slip-up. No sense in being cheap. I'm just going to spend the rest of this money and let Rachael have her way.

The girls help me pick out some things from Old

Navy and Mad Rag. Some heeled boots, crushed velvet tops with the shoulders cut out, jeans ripped at the knee, a few bodysuits (suddenly I'm having Sports Day wedgie nightmares all over again), and skirts. The good thing is that most of the stuff they pick out for me is a reasonable price. When we're done, I have thirty-one dollars to spare.

By the time we get to the movies, our hands are full of bags and there are some other kids from McManus waiting around.

We purchase tickets to see *Midnight's Curse*. As Rachael promised, Bryan is there. So are some other seventh and eighth graders: Sebastian, Leslie, Megan, and Michael. We order popcorn, Twizzlers, and sodas and head to the theater.

I bump into a familiar face walking out of theater number four—John.

I don't know why, but suddenly I feel my whole back fill with sweat. John is with his *abuela* and little brother. He says something to them and walks over to me. I tell Rachael and crew that I'll meet them inside.

"Hey, John. *¡Hola, Señora Lopez!*" I wave at his grandmother, and she waves back.

"Hey, yourself," John says.

We just kind of stand there staring at each other until John breaks the silence. "I see you're racking up in the friends department."

"Oh, Rachael? Yeah, she invited me. You know, just trying to show some of that Welcome to McManus spirit outside of school, I guess."

John doesn't look convinced. "Well, if you say so. Enjoy the movie. It was pretty epic."

Rachael peeks her head out the door to the theater and tells me to hurry it up.

John turns and starts walking toward his family.

"See you at school Monday!" I yell out.

But John doesn't even respond. He just throws up a peace sign and keeps walking.

I make my way inside, and just then I get a text message.

> **Mae**: Hey, stranger. Long time no text. Or Snapchat. Or FaceTime.

The houselights go out. There's no time to text back. Rachael loudly whispers, "Over here, Annabelle! I saved you a seat. "

She saves me a seat all right. Right next to Bryan. And his bright smile and his perfect haircut and his perfect smell.

Woodsy, just like I thought.

I plop into the chair, and the movie begins.

Rachael nudges me in the side. "Aren't you glad I saved you from nerd boy?"

I look at her, confused. "What?"

"Don't act like you don't know what I'm talking about, girl. John is about as dorky as they come. Stick with me, kid. I'll move you up the ranks in no time."

Ranks? I'm not sure how high I want to climb.

31

RETHINKING

Whoever invented bodysuits needs to be put on punishment. No, seriously. By fifth period, I'm so uncomfortable wearing this thing. Also, my feet hurt from the high-heeled booties Rachael picked out for me last Saturday. My mouth is dry from the matte lipstick she made me wear as we *put our faces on* in the bathroom before homeroom. And I'm pretty sure my hair has had enough of being fried every day just to stay straight.

Clairna and John stop me in the hallway just as the lunch bell rings.

"Are you going to come see us practice our band performance for the winter ball?" Clairna asks.

I see Rachael, Natasha, and Lauren coming my way.

"Sure thing, as soon as I'm done eating."

John and Clairna make their way to the gym, lunch

bags in hand. I go to the cafeteria and shyly walk to the table Rachael has claimed as her rightful throne. Bryan is there. He smiles at me, but doesn't say a word. I smile back.

Rachael told me that Bryan wants to ask me to the dance. But other than a smile here or there, it's like he doesn't even know I exist. It doesn't matter anyway because Dad would flip.

"What are you guys wearing to the winter ball?" Natasha kicks off the conversation.

"My favorite color, blue, of course," Lauren says.

Rachael says, "My mom is getting me a ball gown from Luxe in Woodbridge Mall."

I finally speak. "Sounds expensive."

"Four hundred dollars, if you call that expensive. How many times in our lives will we ever have a winter ball? Plus, you wouldn't catch me dead in the same dress more than once."

I think on that for a second. Does that mean I have to go shopping for more clothes? What I purchased with the girls won't last me through the winter at this rate! Maybe I can sneak back to the Second Chance store and find a dress for the winter ball.

Twenty minutes go by of everyone sitting there talking about the dance, how "lit" they're gonna look and how "lit" it's going to be. The whole thing is giving my stomach a case of the heebie-jeebies. Aside from having to dress up, am I going to have to actually dance at this thing?

I decide right then and there that I'm not going. And there's nothing Mom or Dr. Varma can say to convince me otherwise.

Just then, John and Clairna enter the cafeteria, and I can tell they're looking for me. Yikes! I forgot to go to the gym to see them practice.

John boldly walks to Rachael's table. Clairna lags behind.

Rachael stands up first. "Can I help you?"

"I need to talk to Annabelle," John says.

Rachael turns to me as if to ask if that's OK.

"Since when do I need permission to talk to my friend?" John asks.

Rachael sucks her teeth, but I jolt up and say, "It's fine. I'm sorry, John, I forgot."

"Yeah, I bet. You've been forgetting about a lot of things lately. Like who your real friends are."

"I'm her friend too, nerd boy," Rachael says.

Everybody at the table starts laughing.

I want to tell Rachael to stop, but my mouth doesn't let me. Every single part of my face is frozen stiff.

John stands there, waiting to see if I'll do anything. And when I don't, he shakes his head at me, like I'm the biggest disappointment in the world. He walks back to Clairna, and together they leave the cafeteria. I mouth "I'm sorry" at her, but she doesn't even acknowledge me.

Maybe John's right. Maybe I need to rethink this whole friend thing.

32

BLENDING

Things get weirder as the days go on. John, Clairna, and even Nav barely speak to me anymore. My new wardrobe isn't comfortable at all. Like seriously, "cold shoulder" shirts are well . . . cool. Not in a good way! And to make things worse, I'm starting to notice that a lot of the girls at school dress the same. You can barely tell us apart.

Is this really what I want? To be a little soldier in the fashion diva army? To hang out with girls who like to tease my friends?

And for the first time, my inner Daphne and Annabelle become one: *This might not be what you signed up for, girl!*

During science lab, Mr. Friedank pairs us up. In today's experiment we're using rubber bands to test the effects of potential and kinetic energy to help a toy vehicle move.

"Annabelle, your partner will be John," Mr. Friedank says.

John lets out a long sigh and takes his place at the lab table next to me in the front of the class. Mr. Friedank gives further instructions and tells us to begin.

I start gathering the materials we need: K'Nex pieces and varying sizes of rubber bands, but the whole time I don't say anything to John.

There's some giggling coming from the left of our lab table. When I look over, I see it's Rachael and Natasha, and they're staring right at me. I raise my shoulders at them as if to say, "What's going on?" But then they start giggling some more. Rachael rips out a sheet of paper from her notebook and starts writing like a madwoman.

"You ready to work, or are you too busy with your new *squad*?" John asks, taking my attention away from Rachael and Natasha.

"I don't know what you're talking about," I say, snapping a connector to the front axle of the vehicle.

"Well you know what they say?"

"What's that?" I ask.

Mrs. Gironda peeks her head into the classroom and asks Mr. Friedank to step into the hallway for a second. Rachael takes full advantage and flies a paper plane over to my table. I catch it in mid-air, fast before Mr. Friedank walks back in.

"The price of fame is expensive and will leave you broke," John responds.

"Who said that nonsense?" I twist my face and finally look at John. And when I do, the sun catches him right in the eyes, showing off a kaleidoscope of browns, grays, and greens.

"I don't know. I read it in a magazine." He shrugs.

I open the paper airplane, turning my back a little to John so he won't see. And when I see the message, my insides shrivel: *Step away from the dork, Annabelle. We wouldn't want to see you return to dork status.*

"What's with you these days?" John's question breaks me out of my thoughts.

I wonder the same. New clothes. New hair. New "squad." I'm not sure if I'm liking this new me after all.

I take the note, stuff it into my pocket, and glance at Rachael and Natasha, who are laughing uncontrollably now.

"Yeah, we never see you anymore," Clairna chimes in. She and Nav are partnered at the lab table behind us.

"It's like we need an appointment," Nav says.

I turn around, and he bows to me like I'm English royalty.

John throws in one more jab. "Guess we're not good enough for you anymore."

But that's not true! And Clairna pushed me to hang

out with Rachael anyway! Why? So I could get an "in" with Steven Chu, who by the way, suffers from the incurable disease of Immaturitis? After two days of sitting with him at lunch, the diagnosis was easy.

I want to say all of that, but Rachael and Natasha's giggling is throwing my concentration off. And speaking of concentration, it doesn't even look like they've started their project.

"Oh, don't be like that, guys," I whisper. "Besides, Clairna, you made me go shopping with Rachael in the first place!"

"Shopping for clothes is one thing. Shopping for a whole new set of friends is different!"

I don't need to look back to see Clairna give me a major Rachael-level glare.

Ouch.

Mr. Friedank steps back inside the room and paces to our area to make sure we're doing the experiment. John completes the last steps—wrapping a thin rubber band around the toy vehicle back axle eight times to see if it's enough to transform potential energy into kinetic. Four and six winds produced very little movement, if any. But eight times sends the vehicle flying off the lab table.

We record our notes on the lab sheet.

"Excellent work, John and Annabelle," Mr. Friedank compliments.

As soon as Mr. Friedank walks to the back of the lab, John starts up again. "When I first met you, I was like, 'Wow, a girl from Germany who's different and cool and not trying to fit in with anyone.' It's like you didn't have to be phony to make anyone like you."

Then Clairna adds her bit. "You don't need to wear things or hang out with a certain crowd to fit in. We liked you better when you were just yourself."

That last part really hurts, but I don't say anything back, because honestly, what can I say?

Class ends, and John, Clairna, and Nav grab their things and head to next period, leaving me behind.

33

I ALREADY KNOW

My alarm goes off late the next morning. All of my new clothes are in the dirty clothes basket, which means I have to fish out something from my old wardrobe. Or raid Mom's closet, but she's not home to even help me with this fashion emergency.

To make matters worse, the weather gods decided to be comedians today by painting the Linden skies gray with a dash of thunder clouds.

Dad yells from the front door, "Hurry up or I'm going to miss the train. I'll wait for you in the car!"

Quickly, I toss on a pair of brown overalls and a multi-colored plaid shirt. But I need *something* to cuten up the look, so I roll up the pants to my shins and throw on those high-heeled booties. The toaster oven starts screaming just as I draw in one squiggly eyebrow. Next thing I know, I'm flying down the steps to the kitchen, stuffing the burned bagel into my mouth and darting to the car while the weather gods laugh and dump rain on every. Single. Part. Of me.

By the time I get to school, I look a HOT, RAINY, MUDDY POODLE-HAIR MESS!

Rachael and friends waste no time letting me know. "What on earth happened to you, girl?" she greets me in the hallway, her crew around her smirking.

I feel the tips of my ears ignite and stay burning for the rest of the day.

During lunch I walk over to their table and even though there's a spot to sit, Rachael tells me: "Sorry, there's no room."

My inner Daphne voice chimes in: *So let me get this straight. I ditch my friends to hang out with you. I change my fashions and am finally "accepted" by you. And the one day I can't dress to your approval, I'm not good enough to sit with you?*

That's it. I'm done with Rachael.

Of course I don't say any of that. My inner Annabelle won't let me. Being shy can be such a thrill kill sometimes!

So I walk away in a huff. I don't care about trying to walk like some supermodel, and I don't care about wearing clothes that make me look diva-esque and give me wedgies.

Just then I see John, Clairna, and Nav look at me and

then go back to pretending that they're enjoying today's lunch: Veggie Surprise.

LIARS!!!

Clearly, even they don't want me at their lunch table. I'm not sure I can blame them after the way I've been treating them. So I storm out of the cafeteria and go to the next best hiding spot: the paper supply closet.

And Nav is right . . . the smell of new paper is AMAZING!

I pull out my phone and text Mae. Lately, I've been slow to respond to her texts, or I've just not been responding at all. I can handle losing Rachael as a friend, even John, but not Mae.

Me: Hey. Sorry I've been such a bad friend lately.

Two minutes pass. Then five. My heart sinks with the tick of each second that passes. But then . . .

Mae: It's OK, *amiga*! I've been busy too. Working on something big. More on that later. But tell me . . . how is my superstar friend?

I breathe the biggest sigh of relief. At least one friend isn't mad at me. I tell Mae all about this latest Daphne experiment, how annoying the whole fashion thing is, how mean Rachael is, and how I think I've lost the only friends I've made at McManus.

Mae: I think you know what you have to do.

Mae's right. I know exactly how I'm going to fix all of

this. I squeeze my eyes really tight and pray for dismissal to hurry up so this day can be over with already. There's a new vlog waiting to be recorded.

But first, I need to try to make things right.

Belle to Group, John, Clairna, Nav: Hey, guys. I'm sorry. For everything. I'm going back to just being myself. Can we start over and be friends again?

Ten minutes later . . .

seen by all

No response.

34

DAPHNE DOESN'T DO FASHION

As soon as I get home, I transform myself into Daphne—lime green wig with glitter strands, my Harry Potter–style cape, an oversized hat with a feather, and pink-rimmed shades that are about five times too big for my face. I look ridiculous, but I am loving every part of my outfit.

Today I decide I'm going live. Now that my channel has grown to over ten thousand subscribers, YouTube allows this feature. I'm way too anxious about everything that happened at school today to spend time editing in iMovie. I need to get some stuff off my chest before I spontaneously combust.

I set my phone on the tripod, open the app, start playing music and dancing, and I don't even care that I have zero rhythm. Going live in three . . . two . . . one . . .

"Hi, guys! It's your girl, Daphne, and welcome to my channel, *Daphne Doesn't.*

"Today's episode is all about fashion and the top five things I can't stand about following the latest trends:

"Number one: The expense. People of YouTube land, shop the clearance rack! Who spends hundreds of dollars on shoes? Or even better, seventy-five hundred dollars on a coat? Do you realize how many tech gadgets I could get with that kind of money? Thrift shops exist, people. You can probably find that same coat in a thrift shop for *wayyy* cheaper.

"Number two: Rips, rips everywhere! People! Why are we buying purposely ripped clothes? It's cold outside. It's almost Christmas, for crying out loud! So cover up and let it snow, let it snow, let it snow! Geez!

"Number three: Bodysuits. The nineties called, and they want their onesies back! These things need to be a criminal offense. Just trust me when I tell you to *never ever* wear them. Your butt will thank you.

"Number four: Wavy eyebrows. Now I don't mean eyebrows that naturally grow wavy and there's nothing you can do about it. I'm talking about dipping a toothbrush in hair gel to purposely transform your eyebrows into waves that even mermaids would want to swim in. Just . . . don't.

"Number five: And my least favorite one of all?

Blending in. There is no individuality when you're trying to look like everyone else. Where's the fun in that?

"It's cool to be different. It's OK to be yourself. Even if that means some people will make you feel bad about it. So wave your inner fashion weirdo flag high and mighty, because trends may come and go, but individuality lasts forever.

"Thanks for watching *Daphne Doesn't*. Be sure to like, follow, and subscribe. See you on the next episode!"

During the whole taping, I see the views increase. Fourteen hundred and forty-one, then eight thousand, then twenty-seven thousand and counting. The comments are flooding in:

LifeWithDogs: I think following fashion trends is silly too! Just be yourself!

PinkyHearts: Who cares what's on the outside? It's what's inside that matters.

Elle_Sauly: Cool dance moves, Daphne!

BrooklynChica: OMG, please do a vlog just about that silly squiggle-brow!

That last comment sparks an itch to give the people what they want. So I do another live vlog showing everyone just how horrific squiggly eyebrows can look.

And between the two new vlogs, the comments keep rolling in. Funny requests. Positive vibes. All of it makes me feel like what I'm doing means something.

But even though shooting the live vlogs felt like the most amazing release, another familiar feeling soon returns—emptiness. John, Clairna, and Nav haven't responded to my text message, but they all saw it. And now I have a feeling that I blew my shot at real friendship. Because I didn't speak up, I messed it all up. I'm not cut out for school or sports or drama or fashion. But worst of all? I'm not cut out for friends.

It's almost ten o'clock by the time I finish hanging out in my girl cave listening to depressing Ed Sheeran songs.

"Time to close up shop, Annabelle!" Dad yells down the basement steps, just as I'm shutting down my MacBook.

"Coming, Dad."

When I get upstairs, Dad is sitting at the breakfast bar, drinking hot tea. "What's with the glum face?" he asks.

I turn off the basement lights and close the door. Then I pull up a stool and join him at the counter. "It's just things are . . . complicated," I admit.

Dad takes a sip of his tea, and the warm, gingery smell spreads all around the space between us. "I thought things were going well. Aren't you happy? You're Miss Popularity now."

"I'm not sure if any of it matters. The clothes. The fake friends. I felt more like myself when I hung out with John, Clairna, and Nav. Now I think they hate me. And honestly, I'm not sure if I like me like this after all." By the last word, I'm crying.

Dad puts his tea down and pulls me in to his shoulders, where I let it all out. Tears, fears, and a few sobs. "It doesn't matter how other people see you," he says. "All that matters is how you see yourself. As for your old friends, I'm sure things will get better really soon. Say, since Mom's at Fort Dix doing overtime, it's a Daddy-daughter weekend. You know you could invite your friends over, if you want. My kitchen is always open."

My father, Señor Ruben Louis, aka the BEST dad in the world, just gave me an idea. I know exactly how I'll fix things!

35

BEING NORMAL

I go back to school Friday dressed as my normal self. Rachael can have the popularity, the fashion, and the teasing.

As I walk into homeroom, I can feel all eyes on me. And it takes me right back to the first day of school. Counting the tiles on the floor, walking to my seat in the back of the room, hearing the whispers:

"What happened to Annabelle?"

"Looks like she's back to her old self."

"Pick a team, girl. Dope or Dork."

I sink into my chair, trying to block out the comments and the googly eyes. When I do take my eyes off the floor, I notice John staring at me. And not in the *I-still-hate-you* way, but more like a *nice-to-see-the-real-you-again* kinda way.

It starts with a smile, even though it's faint. By second period, it's a casual "hey" from John, Clairna, and then Nav. By third period, it's a "See you at lunch?" from John, which I take as a clear sign that maybe he's not mad at me anymore.

This makes me feel a thousand times better! No more eating in the paper supply closet.

Before lunch, I stop at my locker to switch books. Clairna is at her locker too.

"You sitting with us today, or what?" she says, grabbing her algebra book.

My smile grows and circles around the circumference of my head. "After you guys didn't respond to my text, I thought . . . Listen, I'm sorry if I—"

Clairna holds her hand in the air and cuts me off. "Apologies aren't necessary. I get it. You took a drink from the popular jug. It tasted good at first until that aftertaste settled on your tongue. And I admit, I'm the one who pushed you in that direction, for my own selfish reasons. Turns out Steve Chu has the maturity level of a seven-year-old!"

I start laughing. "I totally agree!"

We slap high fives, and everything feels right in my world again.

"I'll meet you guys in the cafeteria. I have to use the bathroom first."

"Sure thing." Clairna starts making her way to the cafeteria.

When I enter the bathroom, who do I see staring in the mirror, putting her face on?

Rachael stops mid-gloss and tosses the tube into her pink, fuzzy makeup bag. I pay her no mind and handle my business. I take my time, hoping she'll walk out of the bathroom any second now, or that one of her fans will come in and distract her. But under the stall I can see her feet glued in place, like she's waiting for me.

When I'm done, I go to the sink to wash my hands, not looking her way. I wash my hands extra fast, because I just want to get out of there. But then Rachael can't take my ignoring her. She corners me, putting her face so close to mine, I can smell her lip gloss—a mixture of candy canes and something fruity. Must be new.

"Nice outfit, Annabelle."

My soul dies a little, but I refuse to let her see it. "Um, thanks." I inch a little to the left. Rachael follows.

"Check out this YouTube live video." She shoves her iPhone in my face.

I pretend like I'm watching it for the first time.

"Funny, huh?" she asks.

And then she swipes her phone and shows the eyebrow vlog. That's when I know I'm toast.

"Yeah, that girl is pretty hilarious," I say, trying to play it off.

"Hmm . . . so funny because Daphne is showing

the eyebrow trick exactly like the way I showed you," Rachael says.

I don't respond, just kinda nod like, *yeah, that's so crazy, girl!*

But Rachael's not done with me yet. "Say, doesn't that necklace look familiar?" She pauses the video and zooms in.

My hands rise up to my neck. Mom's necklace. The same necklace I forgot to take off last night for my vlog! But there's no way I'm telling Rachael that, so I just lie: "Sort of, I guess. But you can find this necklace at any store. And there's lots of makeup vlogs on YouTube. Daphne could've learned that trick anywhere."

"Oh yeah? Same words and everything, huh? Nice cover-up, Annabelle."

"What do you mean?"

And cue sweaty back!

"It all makes sense now. You, re-enacting the same scene from *Little Shop of Horrors* and then stealing my part from me. Your mom calling you 'Daph'. That YouTube comment about Daphne living right here in New Jersey. And now you're wearing the exact same necklace. I'm not stupid. I know you're Daphne!"

I laugh out loud, trying my best to convince Rachael— and myself—that she's got it wrong. "You've officially lost it, girl."

The second I say that I can't believe it. I've never been so snippy with anyone.

"Nice comeback, dorkface. Way to dodge the accusation."

My stomach hurts because I know I'm about to tell a huge lie.

"It's not me." I can't breathe. My nerves are piling up in my stomach, and any second I'm going to let them all out.

"Well, we'll just see about that, won't we?" Then Rachael storms out of the bathroom.

36

NO MORE HIDING

I can't even think about showing my face in the cafeteria. By now, I'm sure Rachael has told every single one of her friends. And I can't bear the thought of them staring and pointing and whispering. So I do what I've now become an expert at: I hide.

One place I know Rachael wouldn't be caught dead in is the library. Mrs. Ransome, our school librarian, makes this a place where we can really escape. Signs are posted all around: *McManus scholars are building our future!* There are plenty of tables with chairs in the middle of the library and comfortable sofas lining the wall of windows. And to top it off, light classical music plays softly in the background.

Thankfully, the library is almost empty—just two students seated at separate tables and Mrs. Ransome, who greets me with a welcoming smile. I take a seat on the oversized comfy couch in front of the window with the big pine tree. I pull out my MacBook from my knapsack, open up an old video folder, and randomly select one.

I don't notice when John walks in, but I feel his touch when he taps me on the shoulder. "Nice video. Where's it from?" he asks.

It's a clip of Mae and me doing voiceovers, re-enacting a scene from *Star Wars* using action figures. An oldie but goodie.

"I made it myself," I say.

John slides into the seat next to me to take a closer look. I breathe in and catch a whiff of his scent.

Woodsy.

"That's amazing. Your impersonations are spot on. How d'you do that?"

"I can speak in many accents," I say, and then I stop talking because thoughts of Daphne and my perfectly cheeky British accent come up.

"You should make a YouTube channel!" he says.

I take in a large breath. I should tell him the truth before Rachael does. Right now. Stop hiding. Get it over with.

Instead I say, "I'm sorry for not being a better friend." I want to tell him what happened in the bathroom with Rachael, but for some reason I don't.

John scans my face, as though he's waiting for me

to say more. "I know you are. You don't need to hole yourself up in the library or the paper closet every day."

"How'd you know?" I ask.

"Navdeep caught you going in there last week, when *he* was looking for a place to hide."

We burst out laughing. And finally it feels like I have some sense of normal again. But there's that tug in my stomach returning. I've got to say something before Rachael opens her big mouth and starts spreading my secret.

And just when I'm ready to say something, in walk Clairna and Nav.

"We were waiting for you in the cafeteria," Nav says, taking a seat on the carpet.

"Yeah, what happened?" Clairna asks, sitting beside him. "I told you we were cool again. What'd you do? Get nervous?"

I shrug.

Here's my chance to get it all out in front of my friends. But what if they react like Rachael did? Or worse? Then I really will spend the rest of the school year hiding in the paper supply closet.

"Friends again?" John holds out his fist for a bump.

"You got it." I bump fists with him.

It's then that I hear Mae's and Dad's voices echo in my head. Their subtle reminders that things will get better and that they know I'll figure it all out. That's when I come up with a brilliant idea. "How about we have a pizza party tomorrow? My house?" I ask.

Nav's eyes brighten. "Pizza is my favorite food group."

Clairna and John chime in, adding in their favorite toppings. Pepperoni. Mushrooms. Nav adds pineapples. I'm not so sure about that last one.

Just then, Mr. Davis rushes into the library with a box full of posters with snowflakes and other wintry pictures.

"Ah, thank goodness I found you, Annabelle, Clairna! Nicholas Rocco is out sick," Mr. Davis says, before he trips on a section of elevated carpet.

Some of the papers and markers spill out of the box and onto the floor. We all rush to help him pick them up. Mr. Davis breathes a sigh of relief and sits on the couch next to us.

"Am I in trouble or something?" I ask.

"Quite the opposite!" he says. "I need your help. Actually, I can use all the help I can get right now. I tell you, a teacher's work is never done. Last month, it was the play; this month, it's setting up for the Student-Parent Winter Ball. Add in the mounds of history papers I have to grade and the fact that I have two little people at home still in diapers, and I can't tell my right foot from my left foot these days. I digress."

Mr. Davis comes up for air and then continues. "You two did such an amazing job last month building the set for the play, not to mention the double duty of acting in it, Annabelle. I was hoping you could do me a huge favor and help with decorations for the winter ball next week. I'm heading the planning committee."

Clairna springs to her knees, excited about the request. "I'll help!"

Then everyone looks at me, waiting for an answer. I'm hesitant because I have no plans of going to the ball. But then I realize that I wouldn't have to actually *go*, I could just help set it up.

So I say, "Of course I'll help you, Mr. Davis." I turn to my friends. "I guess tomorrow will be a pizza and decorating party?"

Mr. Davis lets out a huge sigh of relief and then hands the box of decorations to me.

"See you guys at six o'clock," I say.

"You got it," John says. "See you then."

Tomorrow, I will hang out with my real friends. No squiggly eyebrows, name-brand jeans, or cherry bomb lip gloss needed.

37

I GOT SOME 'SPLAININ' TO DO

Thank goodness for the weekend. It gives me time to take my mind off of Rachael's drama and set up for my pizza-slash-winter-ball-decorating party with John, Clairna, and Nav. Dad goes easy on me this time. No complaints about boys. He helps me clean the house and decide what pizzas he'll make for my friends: pepperoni for John and me, mushroom for Clairna since she's a vegetarian, and Nav can eat that whole pineapple pizza by himself. Yuck!

The doorbell rings at six o'clock sharp.

"Cool house!" Clairna says as soon as everyone walks in.

"Thanks!" I blush. That reminds me to make sure I shut the door to the basement. I make a mental note to do that in a few minutes.

For the next hour and a half, we settle down at our decorating station in the dining room. We work on all of the decorations from Mr. Davis's box, starting with the snowflakes. There are hundreds of these. We cut them out and use glue to add silver glitter. Next up are the snowmen, which need different patterns and colors for the scarves.

When we're halfway done, Dad heads to the kitchen and fires up the oven to start making the pizzas.

"Dude, your dad is actually making the pizza?" Nav asks.

The delicious smells start to drift from the kitchen to the dining room.

"Oh yeah, no ordering here. Dad does just about everything homemade," I say.

"You should've been here last time with me and Rachael when we worked on our group history project," John says. "He was making Spanish and German food."

My spirit drops when I hear him say Rachael's name, knowing that, come Monday, I will need a plan to deal with her and shut her up once and for all.

Clairna hands me a pair of scissors to cut out the snowmen we've already decorated. "Speaking of Rachael, I've got some scoop!"

Here it comes. I just know it.

"What's that?" John asks.

"The royal queen of McManus is upset that the king of eighth grade didn't ask her out to the winter ball."

"Who? Ahmad Patel?" Nav says. "I'm cool with him. We're in the same karate class, and trust me, he has no interest in her."

"Pizzas are almost done!" Dad yells from the kitchen.

"Smells delicious, Mr. Louis!" John calls out.

"So . . . who are you going to the winter ball with?" Clairna looks straight at me.

And then, it's like the whole world pauses. The holiday music stops playing from the speakers. Nav and John stop cutting snowmen. Dad stops cooking in the kitchen. I can *feel* him listening.

"Um, I'm not going."

John's jaw nearly falls onto the dining table. "What do you mean, not going?"

"Oh come on, Annabelle. You have to go!" Nav says, "Clairna and I are going together . . . as friends."

Clairna smiles shyly.

Dad walks in, as if on cue, wiping his saucy hands on his apron.

"You and John should go to the winter ball *together*!" Clairna says it like it's the brightest idea she's ever had.

I keep cutting, pretending that I didn't hear her, and also that Dad is invisible. I'm expecting him to embarrass me any second. In three . . . two . . .

"That's a good idea, Clairna, especially since parents are invited as well." Dad winks.

Please don't make this moment any weirder than it already is! I stop cutting and look at the floor. And then at John. And there's that smile and that dimple again, sinking all the way to his shiny, brace-covered teeth.

I let out a cough, little at first. But then another one follows and another and another. Clairna hands me a bottle of water. I take a large gulp and let it all sink in.

"If you don't want to go to the dance with me, that's cool. I'm bringing my *abuela* anyway." John shrugs.

"No, no! I want to go," I finally speak. "It's just that I . . . I don't know how to dance."

"That's OK! Neither do I," John says. "I might be the only Puerto Rican on Earth with no rhythm."

Dad starts giggling and points at me. "Make that two."

"Dad!" My cheeks flame up, but I'm laughing too.

"I can show you guys how to dance salsa!" Dad presses a button on the remote, and the stereo switches to a song by Marc Anthony.

He starts moving and twirling to *Vivir Mi Vida* as though he's dancing with Mom, even though she's not here. And then John, Clairna, and Nav join in the dancing.

For the whole song, there they are—my friends and my dad—dancing and laughing as Marc Anthony sings about living your life, through good and bad times.

When the song ends, Dad lowers the volume. "Looks

like you guys are just about done with the decorations. Ready to eat?"

We all scream, "Yeah!" and clear the table to make room for the pizzas.

Dad sends me to the garage to grab more water bottles while he lays out his masterpieces: three homemade pizzas, a tray of fettuccine alfredo, garden salad, and fudge brownies.

When I come in from the garage, I notice it's just Dad and Nav in the dining room.

"Where'd everyone go?" I ask.

Nav points left. "Clairna is washing her hands in the bathroom."

"And I sent John to the . . ." Dad slows every single word, "half bathroom in the basement."

I dart out of the dining room, flames firing up in my ears.

Dad loudly whispers, "SORRY!"

My legs zip to the kitchen, hoping that I'll catch John just in time. But the door to the basement is wide open, the lights on the stairs are in full glow, and John is already in my girl cave.

I huff and puff as I get to my door and find him standing there, touching the rack of Daphne clothes, brushing his fingers across the couch, the sign, the art, every single part that screams I HAVE BEEN LYING!

His back is still turned to me, but I can tell he feels my presence.

"I think I owe you an explanation."

"Well, it's about time."

38

LIFE = RUINED!

"My life is basically over!" I plop myself onto Dr. Varma's couch. After everything that went down these past couple of days, Dad went ahead and called Dr. Varma for an emergency Sunday afternoon appointment.

Outside, the sun is shining, the air is cold, and it smells like the holidays. But inside my therapist's office, I'm not feeling so merry and bright.

"Oh, Annabelle, I doubt your life is over. Your father told me you hit a bump in the road. Why don't we start there?" She invites me to spill it all out, so I do.

"John, Clairna, Nav, and I were asked to be on the decoration committee for the winter ball. So yesterday, I invited them over to work on the decorations and have pizza. John wandered off to the basement, where my girl cave is—aka, where all the Daphne magic happens. So I rushed to find him, hoping I'd catch him before it was too late. Well, I was too late. He stared into my eyes for what felt like years before finally the words spilled out of my mouth: *I can explain*. And you know what he said to me, Dr. Varma?"

"Do tell!"

"'It's about time.'"

And cue the camera! The view zooms in close enough to count the number of freckles on my cheek and the amount of tears building up in each eye—four in the left, two in the right.

Dr. Varma hands me a tissue. "So he knew all along? What gave it away?"

I slump against the back of the couch. "My Daphne wig he found in the bathroom weeks before that. The fact that he knew I could speak in different accents. He even mentioned that I looked like Daphne. And then once he saw the set of my show, it just confirmed everything he already suspected."

I flash back to yesterday, remembering the disappointment on his face and the sincerity of his voice.

"I was really mad at first," he said, "because deep down, I knew you lied. But then I talked to *abuela* about it, and she said that you probably had a good reason to not tell anyone. She said that when you were ready, you'd say something. It's not like everything about you was fake. You're still the cool girl from Germany who can't play sports to save her life!"

I gave John a good slap on the shoulder after that.

"It's just this one small part of you that you're hiding," John said. "You'll figure out the right time to let everyone know."

I swallowed the lump in my throat after all of that. Then John turned off the lights, shut the door to my girl cave, and walked upstairs to the dining room. We ate pizza, had a good time, and he didn't say a word.

Dr. Varma clears her throat, snapping me out of my memory. "Have you told your other friends?"

"Not yet. I thought if I confessed then, it would ruin everything. Does that make me a bad friend?"

"Not at all. But when do you think you'll tell them?"

"Tomorrow at school. Definitely tomorrow, before Rachael gets to them with her big mouth."

"And what about the vlogs? Your fashion video has over fifty thousand views now. Do you think you want to continue?" Dr. Varma asks.

"At this point, I'd say mission accomplished. I've made some friends, who I'd prefer not losing before Mom leaves *forever*. Plus, I'm fresh out of school activities."

"Well if I heard correctly, didn't you mention that you're on the decorating committee for the winter ball? As in dance?" Dr. Varma starts up with that excitement in her voice, and I already know what she's thinking.

Here we go again!

I, Annabelle Louis, do not like sports, can't stand drama, am a complete fashion disaster, and I *definitely* do not dance!

39

DANCING IS NOT FOR ME

One YouTube channel. Three social experiments. And I have hated every! Single! One! But the numbers say otherwise: Sixty-two thousand views. Fifteen thousand subscribers.

Now Dr. Varma is extra pumped for me to keep going!

"I say you go to the winter ball, Annabelle!"

I sigh. "I don't dance, Dr. Varma."

"Oh, but dancing is such a useful skill to have! You'll use it for the rest of your life—" Dr. Varma is interrupted by her buzzer, but she tells me to stay put and invites Dad in to tell him all about her idea for my next vlog.

"So what I'm thinking," she says, after going on and on to Dad and me about all the friends I'll make and the confidence I'll gain, "is that 'Daphne Does Dancing' would be a wonderful vlog to end on!" She claps her hands together in triumph.

To which I respond, "I change my mind. I'm not going to the winter ball anymore."

"Oh, you have to go! Your crush would be *crushed*." Dad laughs at himself, but I don't find anything funny.

"You mean the same guy you didn't even want me hanging out with at first?"

"Oh, I like the kid. Any guy who loves his *abuela* the way he does is fine by me."

"Listen, I'm not one for dancing either, Annabelle," Dr. Varma says. "So how about you conquer your fear of dancing by attending a class? The community center does a free weekly social dancing class. You can even invite your friends."

I picture John, Clairna, Navdeep, and me in tutus twirling around the room and burst out laughing.

"She'll do it," Dad announces.

And just like that, I guess not only am I going to the winter ball, but I'm going to learn how to dance and share it with my YouTube followers. Hooray. Can't you just hear the excitement in my voice?

40

BACK AT SCHOOL

Today's mission? Find Clairna and Nav ASAP! I look for them as soon as I get to homeroom Monday morning, but they're nowhere to be found. Not even John is around. Apparently, the band will be practicing in the gym all morning. The winter ball is coming up Friday, and there isn't much time left to get all of the songs they'll be performing memorized perfectly. But I have no idea where Nav is.

Right before the first-period bell rings, Mr. Davis gets on the loudspeaker and announces: "Will the winter ball decorating committee report to the gym during lunch?"

Perfect. I'll see them then and get this confession over with once and for all!

Rachael stares at me all through homeroom, and I sit there feeling her eyes pierce holes in me, waiting for her to say something. But she doesn't.

I get through the morning periods without so much as Rachael saying one word.

The rain starts up right before lunch. No outdoor recess today, which means some students will trickle their way into the gym to hang out. I grab some of the decorations from my locker and zip down the halls to get there first.

Nav is waiting when I arrive.

"Where were you this morning? I've been looking for you," I say.

"Doctor's appointment. My parents just dropped me off. The band is just finishing up," he says, "then we can start taping the snowflakes to the walls."

I find my friends nestled in the band on stage. John is on the trumpet. Clairna is on the clarinet. She spots me and waves just as the band plays the final note of "Walking in a Winter Wonderland."

Mr. Reyes directs the band to stand up and take a bow. "Excellent work!" he says. "Practice will be again tomorrow morning during homeroom, and first and second periods. You may go, but don't forget to take your instruments with you."

Then Mr. Reyes gathers his things and exits the stage. Big mistake! Kids are starting to pour into the gym, and they're bringing in a lot of noise.

I see Rachael come in alone, like a one-woman show. Our eyes meet, and the slyest smile grows on her face.

Quickly, I place the box of decorations on the floor and ask Nav to follow me. I run up onto the stage where John and Clairna are packing up their instruments.

More kids pour into the gym, a few of them bouncing basketballs.

"What'd you think of our performance, Annabelle? It was *lit*, right?" Clairna asks.

"Yeah, totally. But guys, can we go in the hallway? I want to talk to you about something."

"Oh, about the social dance class? John mentioned you wanted to invite us to it tomorrow night. I'm in!" Clairna says.

"Sounds fun . . . and embarrassing!" Nav says.

John snaps his fingers as if to say, "You better hurry up and say something!"

Rachael is drawing closer, down the aisle. And now she's got a few of her friends trickling in behind her.

"Just who I was looking for! Hello, *Daphne*!" Rachael says loudly.

The kids stop playing basketball. Rachael's friends look at each other in pure confusion.

I scan the room for Mr. Davis, Mr. Reyes—really any teacher to magically appear and tell Rachael to shut up and for everyone else to sit quietly on the gym floor.

But who needs a teacher? Rachael's large and in charge and has everyone's attention.

She inches closer to the stage, where I'm standing with my three *amigos*, behind the microphone . . . that's apparently still on. *Thanks, Mr. Reyes.*

The sound of my pounding heart can be heard. That I am sure of.

"What did you just call her?" Clairna asks while I turn into a shriveling pile of dust.

Rachael places her hands on the stage floor and then vaults herself on it to stand with us. Meanwhile the crowd gathers and moves closer, eager to see the show.

"Oh, you heard correctly. I called her Daphne." Then she faces the audience with her arms spread out like wings. "Ladies and gentlemen of McManus, allow me to introduce you to the one, the only . . . the biggest liar in school, Daphne, YouTube star of the vlog *Daphne Doesn't!*"

Rachael is in her element now, with her shoulders rounded out and the biggest, meanest smile planted on her face. Meanwhile, my heart is pounding at top speed, and I'm looking for something, anything, to say.

The whispers from the audience begin.

"Is she for real?"

"Annabelle is a little weird . . . just like Daphne."

"They kind of look alike."

"No, they don't! Annabelle's from Germany. Daphne is British!"

My heart is in full panic attack mode. In and out, my chest heaves. John, Clairna, and Nav stand there waiting for me to say something. Clairna steps in. "You don't know what you're talking about. I watch that show, and Annabelle is nothing like Daphne!"

Then Nav steps in. "I think you're wrong about this one, Rachael. You're just trying to stir up drama, like always."

Something comes over Clairna, and she turns into someone I've never seen before. "Yeah, *girlfriend*, your braids must be too tight."

That sends the whole audience into a frenzy.

"Whoa!"

"She roasted you!"

"Can't come back from that!"

Rachael's whole face drops. She places her hands on her hips and gives Clairna the death stare.

Clairna raises her hand to slap me a high five. It's the weakest high five ever on my part. "I'm tired of this girl thinking she can just bully people," she mutters.

Rachael lifts her finger in the air, prompting everyone to shut up once again. The power this girl has, I tell you!

"Use your brains, doofuses!" she begins. "Annabelle started school a few weeks after we'd already been here. She comes from Germany and speaks all these languages, so accents probably aren't a big deal for her. And how funny is it that I caught her reciting the same lines from that same 'Daphne Does Drama' video? I even heard her mom slip and call her *Daph*! And then in her last video, she wore that same necklace. . . ." Rachael looks me over frantically. "Where's the necklace, dorkface?"

Everyone is staring at me, and I can't take one more second. This is it. I have to say something . . . now.

So I step closer to Rachael, near the microphone. "Rachael is right. . . ." The whole audience gasps. "Sort of," I add. "I know Daphne."

Some of the kids in the audience start jumping and clapping. Even Clairna looks amused.

Then I add one more lie to seal the deal, "She's my cousin."

That makes everyone scream except for two people. John and Rachael.

I can't even bear the look of disappointment on John's face. That's two strikes now.

"If Daphne the YouTube star is your cousin, prove it. Bring her to the dance. I saw the YouTube comment. She lives right here in Jersey!" Rachael says loud and clear on the mic.

Someone from the audience screams, "DO IT!"

Then another person joins, "DO IT!"

Next thing I know every. Single. Student. Is chanting. *"DO IT! DO IT! DO IT!"*

Mr. Davis walks in from the back of the auditorium.

"Hey, what's all the commotion about?" He joins the crowd near the stage, and everyone quiets down.

"Annabelle is related to that famous YouTube star from *Daphne Doesn't!*" Clairna shouts, then she turns to me. "And holy moly, why didn't you tell me, girl?"

I don't have an answer for that, other than a shrug and a fake smile.

Rachael jumps in. "Annabelle told us that she's bringing Daphne to the winter ball."

My imaginary camera zooms in to Rachael's eyes and the special effects make them glow red. I know that Rachael is waiting for me to fall apart right there so she can prove her point and further embarrass me.

"Why, that's GREAT!" Mr. Davis yells, and everyone starts up all over again. "We can have her perform for us!"

The kids hop up onto the stage and circle me, pushing Rachael back farther and farther away from me. Her face looks angrier by the second as even her groupies surround me and hug me, saying:

"Oh my god, I can't wait to meet your cousin. This is going to be so cool."

"Annabelle, you're going to be the most popular girl in seventh grade."

"No way! Make that in the WHOLE school."

That sends Rachael stomping off the stage, down the steps, and to the double exit doors. But not a single person notices. The knots in my stomach return as I see John's face, knowing the real secret that lies between us. But for that one moment it sure does feel good to see Rachael crumble to ashes for a change.

41

MONE-WHO?

"Annabelle, come upstairs, please. We need to talk!" Dad yells as I'm hanging out in my girl cave.

That sends a shiver down my spine. I didn't tell him what happened in school today with Rachael.

"Yes, Dad."

He's sitting at the kitchen table with dinner spread out for us: pepper steak, baked potatoes topped with sour cream and chives, and a garden salad. Dad could give those chefs on the Food Network a run for their money!

"Have a seat. Let's have dinner together. I want to show you something."

The front door slams just as we dig in. Mom's been working double shifts lately, preparing for her TDY to Afghanistan.

"Smells good, Ruben. I was dreaming about your food all the way up the turnpike." Mom washes her hands at the kitchen sink and joins us at the table.

Dad holds up a piece of paper. "You will never believe the email I received today about your Daphne channel."

"What is it?" I ask, confused.

"Because a number of your viewers have either watched or clicked on the ads featured in your videos, your channel has reached monetization status."

Mom starts choking on her steak and quickly reaches for water. I'm mid-bite, trying to translate whatever language Dad just spoke in.

"What does that mean?" I ask between chews. "Mone-who?"

Mom snatches the paper out of Dad's hand and starts breathing loudly.

"*Schätzchen, mi amor!*" Mom screams. "It means your channel made some money, honey!"

Now I'm snatching the paper out of Mom's hand and reading through the email. My eyes dart straight to the numbers, the comma, and the ZEROS. Far more than any allowance I've ever gotten! Tension builds in my shoulders. I toss the paper away from me like it's some contagious disease.

What the heck am I supposed to do with all of that money? Daphne was supposed to be just an experiment. I didn't ask to be viral or famous or rich!

Dad and Mom each grab one of my hands to calm me down.

"We need to talk about what to do with this money. It's not millionaire status, but at a couple thousand dollars, it's bound to keep increasing," Dad says.

"Sweetie," Mom says, "I'm not going to tell you what to do. This is your choice."

Lots of thoughts flood my brain. How am I supposed to handle all of this pressure? And my big fat lie! How am I supposed to continue to be a regular kid by day and a YouTube star by night? And now there's money involved too? I guess most kids would be screaming, *Take the money and run!* But suddenly I don't feel good anymore. I leave half of my plate uneaten, which is a first for me, especially when it comes to Dad's cooking.

"May I be excused?" I ask.

"Of course," Dad says.

I walk upstairs to my room, close the door, and drift off into a sleep where YouTube and vlogs and fans and money don't exist.

42

TOO COOL
FOR TUTUS

John and Clairna are already waiting for me when I get
to the community center the next night for our dance
class.

"Where's Nav?" I ask.

"He texted that he couldn't make it. He forgot he had
karate tonight."

The class is packed with a lot of people . . . old people.
We're literally the youngest ones there.

The teacher is a tall, ballerina-thin woman with a
tight bun and a thick Russian accent.

"My name is Madame Anastasia, and today . . . we
dance!" She holds her arms out in a ballet position.

"Um, Annabelle, what in the world have you signed
me up for? Is this ballet?" John mutters through clenched
teeth.

"Ballet is your first dance style of the night," Madame Anastasia announces. "Now, everyone, pick your shoes and tutu and let's get started!"

In front of the glass mirrors, there are two bins. One is piled high with used ballet shoes rubber banded together in pairs. The other is overflowing with tutus in pink, white, and black.

John throws his hands in the air and huffs at me, "You gotta be kidding, right?"

"Hurry along!" Madame Anastasia calls out, forcing the three of us into military stance.

I give John a look that says *I'm super sorry*, while Clairna snorts loud enough for the whole class to hear.

There's no turning back now. We make our way to the bins to get ballerina-fied. But the old folks beat us to the bins, taking the best and leaving behind scraps. A black tutu for Clairna, a pink one for me, and John also gets a pink tutu because it's the only one left.

My stomach rumbles with laughter as soon as he puts it on. Clairna looks ready to burst out laughing too. And there we are: three *amigos* dressed in poofy tutus and ballet shoes, each one of us looking more ridiculous than the next.

John gives us the death stare. It doesn't take a genius to know he's thinking: *You tell anyone about this, and you will feel my wrath!*

Everyone else in the class is so serious. They're standing at the barre stretching and warming up. We file in line to join them.

Madame Anastasia claps her hands twice, getting everyone's attention. Then she begins to pace the room as she speaks. "As many of you already know, ballet is the foundation of all social dance forms. This is why we begin tonight's class with ballet. It takes precision, technique, and—"

WHACK! Madame taps John on the butt with her pointer.

"Oww!"

"Posture!" She leans into his face, and I'm sure I see her eyes glow fiery red.

Poor John! But Clairna and I are dying by this point!

Madame reviews all of the ballet positions with us, first through fifth. And then she teaches us some basic moves like arabesque, pique turns, and plié.

I move through the steps in true Annabelle style: dangly, wet-noodly legs and arms that refuse to listen to anything Madame Anastasia is saying. She says, "Feet together," my feet say, "Nice try, lady!" No matter how hard I try, my body does the opposite.

After the twelfth posture correction, Madame Anastasia throws me a shady, "Be sure you come back again next week. We'll need lots more classes."

She walks to the other side of the room to check on the other dancers' forms.

"I can't even begin to tell you guys how silly we look right now," I whisper through a demi-plié.

"Seriously plotting your demise right now, Annabelle!" John grunts as he lifts on his toes to relevé.

Clairna's whole face is red now from holding in her laughter. "Trust me, we won't be doing any of these kind of moves at the dance on Friday."

When she says the word dance I feel a twinge in my whole body. I'm supposed to bring "Daphne" to the winter ball, and I still haven't told Clairna and Nav the truth. This tiny voice inside me says it's not the right time. I'll wait until I have them both together, in private.

"Good job, class!" Madame orders us to take off our tutus and ballet slippers. "The next style we learn is the ballroom classic waltz, a dance that requires you to be light on your feet and move with grace! Now, partner up!"

Everyone finds a partner except me. There are an odd number of students in the class.

Madame Anastasia comes over to us and says, "You three will work together. You, sir," she says to John, "begin with her." She points to Clairna.

Madame shows the class the moves and counts.

"Sway your body to the left! Point your toes forward! Don't forget to end in the promenade position!"

For me it goes in one ear and out the other.

When Madame tells us to switch partners, Clairna says, "This will be good practice for you. Rachael is going to be so jealous when she sees you dancing like the belle of the ball. I can't wait to see the look on her face."

My stomach makes this loud gurgling noise, but then Madame Anastasia turns on the music, which thankfully covers up the sound.

"How much longer before you tell her that you're really Daphne?" John whispers.

"I need more time," I say, stepping on his toes.

"Ouch!"

"Sorry about that." My feet turn outward like a duck's, and I try my best to keep up with John, who is clearly much better at this waltz thing than I am.

"Well, don't take too long."

For the final dance, Madame says she has a guest teacher who will show us how to do hip-hop line dances.

"Ladies and gentlemen, I introduce to you master hip-hopper, JT!"

The whole class goes wild when this guy walks in. If I didn't know any better, I'd think he was on one of those dance shows I've seen on television.

JT says we'll learn three line dances: the Cha-Cha Slide, the Wobble, and the Dougie. But first he shows us the moves for each dance.

Boom boom, kat, ske dee dow!

That's literally how he teaches the moves. No counting. Just shouting out these words as he dips and slips and slides. To me, none of it makes any sense. But John and Clairna already know all the moves. They've both done these dances plenty of times at weddings and birthday parties.

The music begins and the singers tell us what to do—sort of—slide to the left, slide to the right. But everything is going so fast, and I start bumping into the other dancers. Meanwhile everyone is getting down with their bad selves like a bunch of professional back-up dancers!

Two hours later, the torture—I mean *dance class*—is finally over. Yet another meaningless experiment brought on by Dr. Varma. I'm starting to think this woman doesn't know what she's doing.

43

DAPHNE VLOGS ABOUT DANCING

As soon as I get home, I retreat to my girl cave. The whole world needs to know just how pointless dancing is. I throw on an outfit from the clothing rack, along with an orange wig styled in a bun, and a *Phantom of the Opera* mask. I look fabulously ridiculous.

I blast a playlist of Beyoncé, Demi Lovato, and Lady Gaga, and let the music take over. Going live in *three . . . two . . . one . . .*

"Hey, guys. It's your girl, Daphne, and I'm here with your latest episode of *Daphne Doesn't*. Today's topic? Dancing. Here are the top five reasons I definitely don't dance:

"Number one: It's just awful. Yeah, I said it. Sorry, not sorry! People moving and sweating and bumping into each other? Not for me!

"Number two: My school is having a dance, and honestly, I don't want to go. I'd prefer to be anywhere else than at school for longer than I have to be. Not only do I have to wake up early to go to school and work hard all day, I'll have to come home, shower, and change into some itchy, cutesy outfit, just to go back to school and hug the wall for three more hours. Why? Because I CAN'T dance! No thanks. I'd rather stay home.

"Number three: Line dances are the WORST! My poor dance teacher tried his best to teach me how to become a professional "Dougie-ist," but that was an epic fail. I'm sorry, but people look silly trying to do the Dougie. And don't get me started on the Wobble!

"Number four: The Cha-Cha Slide has WAY too many instructions! Slide to the left? Slide to the right? Drop it to the floor and try not to break your knees getting up? It's bad enough that I have to listen to instructions all day at school! I'll save myself the torture and stay away from the dance floor!

"Number five: Last but not least, I'd like to go on record saying that ballet is the most evil of all dance forms! The expectation compared to the reality is way off! Expectation? You're dressed in your pretty tutu with your perfect ballerina bun, doing the most perfect grand jeté! Reality? You look like a sweaty dog, leaping for a Frisbee while playing in the park with your human.

"So there you have it, people. The top five reasons why I definitely don't dance. Sure, it's easy to say that with a little effort, and maybe even a few dance classes, anyone can learn how to dance. I don't agree with this at all. I think dancing is a natural ability. It's probably best to acknowledge when you're just not good at something so you can make the time to find what you're really good at. Which in my case is NOT dancing!"

The drum beat kicks in louder. I throw my leg high in the air, try my best to do a grand jeté leap, and tumble down to the floor.

"See what I mean? Don't forget to like, share, subscribe, and comment."

The love pours in throughout my live video:

LizaBooxoxo: This might be your funniest video yet.

CheerTay245: You might have given yourself a concussion with that last dance move. That's why I don't dance either!

OfficialNena13: Daphne is coming to my school dance! It's going to be LIT!

44

BLAST FROM
THE PAST

Ever since the Daphne announcement, the other students have been following me everywhere I go. And when I say everywhere, I mean *every*where. They're at my locker, stuffing themselves at our lunch table—not even complaining about its proximity to the garbage can—and this one kid had the nerve to slip a note under my stall door while I was using the bathroom: *So do you think you can get your cousin to autograph this for me?*

It was a crumpled-up tissue. I didn't stay long enough to see if the boogers came included.

Between that and the constant "How does it feel to be related to someone famous?" comments, I think I've had enough.

And apparently, so has Rachael. Her queen status has been demoted.

When the dismissal bell rings, I dart out of the front

doors, searching for Mom's car. It just so happens that Rachael is walking out the door at the same time. She looks at me but doesn't say anything. Everyone's rushing to the bus, but not her.

"You're not taking the bus today?" I ask her.

"Don't try to be nice to me now," she snaps.

We both stop walking and face each other while hundreds of students race out of the school like it's on fire.

"Me? You're the one who started all of this drama!" I say.

"Well, all you had to do was admit the truth. Instead you just made the lie bigger and made me look like a liar, when really *you're* the liar." Rachael rolls her eyes, but then gazes past me. "Wait. Why is my mom talking to your mom?"

I whip my head around, and sure enough there are our two moms, hugging each other by their cars.

Rachael and I race past the students and the buses to intervene.

"Mom, we gotta hurry up and go," she says nervously.

"Umm, yeah, me too. Mom, let's get out of here," I say.

"Rachael, don't be so rude. Put your things in the car and come meet an old friend of mine!"

Rachael tosses her backpack into the car, slams the door shut, and walks to the driver's side, where both our moms are standing. Mom gives me a look that says, *you'd better get yourself over here too.*

I take a deep breath and follow Rachael, nervous smile and all.

Mom starts, "Rachael, I didn't know that your mom was the one and only Sharon Wright, Linden High Basketball star!"

Rachael's mom whips her dreadlocks to the side and starts laughing. "Hey now!"

"So you two went to school together?" I ask.

"Nice to meet you, Annabelle, and we sure did!" Rachael's mom holds out her hand for me to shake it.

Rachael coughs and says *Daph* under her breath. No one catches it but me.

"It's good to meet you too, Mrs. Myers," I say.

"Oh, it's back to Ms. Wright." Rachael's mom then mutters to mine, "The divorce was finalized last year."

Rachael shrinks about three inches toward the ground. That's when I do the math in my head. She told me her dad was deployed almost a year ago. The divorce must have happened around the same time. Talk about a double whammy!

"I'm sorry to hear about that. You and Mike were Linden High's magic couple," Mom says.

"Well, sometimes the magic doesn't last. But you know what? I'm real glad to see you back in Linden after all these years. Now our girls can grow up together and be the best of friends like we were."

I gulp an imaginary sip of shame juice. By the looks of it, Rachael's drinking from the same cup. The last word we'd probably use for each other right about now is "friend."

"Let's not speak in past tense anymore," Mom says. "We gotta reconnect, girl. And hopefully sooner than later because I'm leaving after Christmas for a six-month assignment in Afghanistan."

Now I'm the one shrinking to the ground, because for the past three months I've tried to wipe away that thought. Pretend that the moment will never come, even though time is flying.

Ms. Wright gasps, reaches for me, and pulls me in for a hug.

"Oh, we're gonna look out for your baby girl while you're gone. You have our word. Right, Rachael?" Everyone's eyes shift to Rachael, who nods reluctantly.

"I really appreciate that, Sharon," Mom says.

"It's too bad you guys didn't move here last year. Rachael had it bad when her dad first left. Changed her whole attitude!"

"Mom!" Rachael says, flames flying from her mouth.

But Ms. Wright just swings her hand in the air and pays Rachael no attention.

"Deployment can be hard on children, I know. That's why we've been taking Annabelle to see a therapist to help her prepare for my trip."

Now I'm the one saying, "Mom!"

"Oh hush, there's nothing wrong with being able to express your feelings."

"You got that right!" Ms. Wright and Mom link their hands together.

"There was this camp I wanted to send Rachael to last summer. It's just for military kids whose parents have been or are currently deployed. But with everything that went on with the divorce and finding a new place to live, the expense was too much."

By now, I see water forming in Rachael's eyes. And she looks nothing like the cool, fashion-savvy, diva leader of McManus that I'm used to seeing. The girl standing next to me is . . . empty.

I understand now. The mood swings. The teasing. The random moments of sadness. The deployment. The effort to put on a brave face and pretend like everything is perfect, when in reality, nothing is.

And there's that tug in my stomach again. And that curious voice that wonders what I could do to change all of that for Rachael, but also for me too.

Without anyone seeing, I take my index finger and poke Mom on the arm.

Code for: "I need to leave now."

Also code for: "I need some time to think through my feelings."

Dr. Varma would be proud that I haven't spontaneously combusted.

Mom gives Ms. Wright a hug. "Let me get this girl home so she can get her homework done. I'll see you at the winter ball?"

Ms. Wright says that she'll be attending the ball with Rachael. The four of us part ways and head to our cars.

Mom starts the engine and turns the heat on full blast. "What a blast from the past, huh?" she says.

"Mom . . ."

"Yes?"

"I can do whatever I want with that YouTube money?"

"Whatever you want."

45

TEXTING MAE IN THE UK

As soon as I get home, I blast through my homework—twenty fraction word problems and a reader's response sheet to Langston Hughes' poem, "Dreams."

I get a notification on my phone from YouTube. My last video, "Daphne Definitely Doesn't Dance" hit one hundred fifty thousand views! In my mind, I see the dollar signs adding up. Most kids would be pumped about this, but not me. If I've learned nothing else from Dr. Varma's social experiments, it's that I could care less about being rich or famous.

I wrap up my homework and start searching the Internet to flesh out my plan. It doesn't take long to find what I'm looking for. Everything I need is right there. The information, the person in charge, and the contact phone number.

My phone beeps again. It's a text from Mae. Perfect

timing. I tell her all about my plan for the YouTube money, and I can hear her scream her response right through the text:

> **Mae**: Really? Are you sure that's what you want? You're a much better person than me!
>
> **Me**: It's the right thing to do.
>
> **Mae**: Well since you're in the mood for surprises, I'll have one for you real soon.
>
> **Me**: Oh come on, you've been keeping me in suspense for weeks!
>
> **Mae**: You'll just have to wait a little longer, *amiga*!

I finish up my texting with Mae, shut down the lights in my girl cave, and head upstairs to have dinner with Mom and Dad. Dad strikes again with another chef-quality meal: crab-stuffed salmon, garlic mashed potatoes, and steamed broccoli. My lips are dragging on the floor by the time I reach the table.

Halfway through dinner I announce, "I surfed the Internet and found what I was looking for. This is what I want to do with the money."

Then I slide the printout across the table to my parents for them to take a look. They sit in silence reviewing the paper.

"How much?" Dad grabs his glass to take a sip of water.

"All of it," I respond.

Dad almost chokes. Mom smiles and fights back her tears. "That's my girl."

46

THE DRAMA RETURNS

It's the day before the dance. Nav, John, Clairna, and I decide to meet in the auditorium during recess to put the finishing touches on the decorations. The final piece we have to make is the blue and white balloon arch. We blow up so many balloons, and with each one I feel the tension creeping up in my shoulders. It's just the four of us in the auditorium. Mr. Davis ran to the office to make some copies.

"I don't care how weird I look dancing tomorrow. I'm gonna dance the night away." Nav does some robotic move, and John and Clairna start laughing.

"I'm so excited. Mom's pulling me out of school a little early so I can get my hair and nails done. What are you gonna wear, Annabelle?" Clairna asks.

This is the moment I've been waiting for. "I'm dressing up . . . as Daphne." I say the last two words almost like a whisper.

Nav leans in. "Like who?"

"Why would you want to dress up like your cousin?" Clairna fills a balloon with air.

"She's not," John says.

The balloon slips from Clairna's lips and swirls all the way to the floor.

"Not what? Not coming?" Nav looks at John for answers.

John shakes his head. "My name is Bennett, and I ain't in it." He continues to place the balloons on the arch.

"I've been lying to you guys," I say.

Clairna's jaw drops lower with the passing of each second. Nav just kind of stands there looking like he doesn't know what to do with his arms.

"Girl, I am not following you. So your cousin isn't coming?" She snaps her fingers together. "Darn, I *so* wanted to rub that in Rachael's face!"

I scan my brain for the right words. "No, it's just that—Daphne is . . . *me*."

Nav doubles over and starts laughing. "So you're your own cousin? What kind of freaky joke are you trying to tell?"

John finally stops building the arch and throws me an anchor. "Guys, what Annabelle is trying to say is that her real name is Annabelle *Daphne* Louis. She's Daphne, the YouTube star."

Clairna and Nav don't say anything for a second, but it doesn't take long for Clairna to show how she really feels about my keeping a secret. "You've been lying to us this whole time?" Her voice is a good three pitches higher than before.

"Why didn't you just tell us from the beginning?" Nav says. Then he looks at John, disappointment all over his face. "And you kept it from us too?"

"Wait, you told John before you told me? I thought I was your girl, Annabelle!" Red surfaces on Clairna's whole face.

"This isn't John's fault," I say. "He was just trying to be a good friend."

"Well, that makes one of us!" Clairna says.

"I can explain. All of this was an experiment to try new things at school as a way to make friends, since I was new here."

"So that's what we are to you, *Daphne*? An experiment?" The words jump out of her mouth like a pack of knives.

"You guys aren't an experiment. You were the first friends I made here. It's just that once I started getting popular, I felt like if I said anything about the YouTube thing you wouldn't want to be my friends anymore."

"Well, you got that part right!"

"Are you gonna tell?" I ask.

"You can have your experiments and your fans and your lies! I'm sure you'll figure out how to let everyone else down." Clairna storms out of the auditorium, and Nav runs after her.

And my tears start up all over again. "What am I supposed to do now?"

John hands me a tissue from his pocket. The tears are coming out thick and fast. I wipe my eyes with it, trying my best to stop the flow, but it doesn't work.

"Now you find a way to tell the truth . . . to everyone."

"But how?" I ask.

John scratches a patch of hair on his head, but doesn't offer a response.

"I understand if you don't want to be my friend anymore either," I say.

John places his hand on my shoulder. "I'm not going to let you go through all of this by yourself."

"But everyone is expecting me to show up tomorrow with my cousin Daphne. Clairna and Nav hate me. Rachael hates me. Meanwhile thousands of people in YouTube land think I'm the greatest thing ever, but those people aren't real. You guys are. Basically this whole experiment is one big failure."

Just then Mr. Davis walks in, in the best mood ever. "Tomorrow's the big day, guys! Ah, it looks like a winter wonderland in here!" He skips and sings his way up to the stage where we're standing.

I turn my back so he doesn't see the red in my eyes.

John says, "We're all done with decorations, Mr. Davis. If you don't mind, we'll head back to class."

I look around the gym. It's done, but it's not to my full liking. But none of that matters because I don't have the energy to blow one more balloon.

"Where are we going?" I ask John.

"Do you have your cell phone and your laptop on you?"

"Yeah, but why?"

"You're going to the dance tomorrow . . . as Daphne. It's time for one final experiment."

47

A REASON TO SMILE

Mae: How does Christmas with your BFF sound?

Me: What are you talking about?

Mae: Effective Monday, the Tanakas are taking on the Big Apple, New York City. We'll be on holiday for two weeks!

Me: STOPPPP!

Mae: So you don't want to see me?

Me: Wait, no! Omg. Of course I do! This is the best news I've heard all year.

Mae: You ready for the dance tonight, *amiga*?

Me: Ready as I'm gonna be.

48
THIS IS IT

Mom helps me get dressed for the dance. I choose a Victorian-style winter white dress with lace and ruffles, along with a white and silver wig and the mask from my last video.

"I think you're doing the right thing, sweetie. I'm so proud of you," Mom says as she puts blush on my cheeks.

Dad knocks on the door and peeks his head in. "John and his *abuela* are here."

When I get to the stairs, John is waiting for me, standing next to his grandmother. In his hands he holds two rose corsages. It's like a scene straight out of Cinderella. John is dressed in a black suit with a silver tie to match my silver and white wig.

"*Tan lindos!*" his grandmother squeals, calling the two of us beautiful.

I glide down the stairs, and John places one corsage

on my wrist and then one on his grandmother's. Then he takes a bow. "Are we ready for a fun night?" he asks.

"I guess." I shrug my shoulders.

Mom and Dad grab their coats, and we all head to the car.

McManus is lit up on the outside with holiday lights and the streets are full of parked cars. People are standing out in the cold, with signs in their hands that say, "Welcome to McManus, Daphne!"

I want to scream and tell Mom to turn the car around and drive us back home, apologize to John's *abuela* for ruining what supposed to be a "night out on the town" for her. But I can't say any of it. Not now. Seeing the excitement on John's face, I try to ignore the fear I feel.

The flashing lights blind me as soon as I step out of the car.

"Whoa, I wasn't expecting all of this!" Dad jumps out of the passenger side and comes around to grab me. He takes his arm and wraps it around me while people are screaming:

"Oh my goodness! It's Daphne, guys!"

We push our way through the crowd with Mom, John, and his *abuela* sticking close behind us. When we finally get in, I see Mr. Davis waiting for us. He gets all excited and says, "Welcome to McManus, Daphne!

We're so lucky to have you here at the ball. Say, where's your cousin, Annabelle?"

Everybody is silent, looking at me.

I clear my throat and throw on my British accent.

"Well I . . ."

"Oh, no worries! Knowing Annabelle, she's probably checking to make sure the decorations are to her liking. I tell you, Mr. and Mrs. Louis, your daughter is quite the perfectionist!"

Dad and Mom flash Mr. Davis their best smiles.

"We're going to open the doors soon and get the party started. But first I want to make sure that you have everything you need, John. You mentioned something about the projector screen?" Mr. Davis asks.

John's eyes grow wide. "Yes! Let me make sure everything is set up now before you open the doors."

"Ooh, are we going to see a new episode of *Daphne Doesn't*?" Mr. Davis asks.

John and I look at each other.

"Um, something like that," I say.

Mom, Dad, and John's *abuela* make their way to the snack and punch table in the back of the gym.

I follow John backstage to help him set up.

The band members are let in early, along with Mr. Reyes, the band director. I see Clairna walk in just as John readies himself to leave me alone. She's wearing a red velvet dress with a black belt and black shoes. Her hair is styled in big cluster curls with a Santa hat to complete the look.

She. Looks. Amazing.

"I'll come back here when it's time. Will you be OK?" John asks.

"Sure," I say, though I'm not sure one bit.

Then John does the strangest thing. He hugs me. For five seconds longer than a *that's-just-my-buddy* level hug. I don't know what to do with my hands. Wrap them around his back? His neck? How do they do it in those teen rom-com movies again? It's all too much to think about, so I just stand there with my arms dangling at my sides until the moment is over.

He pulls away, winks at me, and then takes his position on stage with the rest of the band. Mr. Davis starts to open the doors and the band plays "Walking in a Winter Wonderland" as the students run into the gym, screaming, with their parents trailing behind them. A few more songs—"Deck the Halls" and "Jingle Bells"— and their performance is complete.

"Ladies and gentlemen, boys and girls, let's hear it for the McManus Middle School band!" Mr. Davis announces on the microphone.

Just then, I see Nav enter the gym with his parents. Then Rachael and her mom. I'm behind the curtains so she doesn't see me, but I can already tell who she's looking for . . . Daphne.

The DJ starts to play "I've Got a Feeling" and everyone heads to the dance floor. Halfway through the song, the kids start chanting: "DAPHNE! DAPHNE! DAPHNE!"

Mr. Davis runs to the stage and taps the microphone. "Is this thing on?"

The DJ lowers the music.

Everyone starts cheering wildly.

"I believe this is the moment we've all been waiting for. The whole school's been buzzing about our special guest all week. Let's bring up two very special ladies to the stage: McManus's very own Annabelle Louis and her cousin, Daphne, the YouTube star of the hit vlog *Daphne Doesn't!*"

I inhale a deep breath in the middle of everyone screaming and take one step, then another, and another. Soon I emerge from behind the curtain.

Everyone is clapping except Rachael, Clairna, and Nav, whom I spot right away in the crowd.

I clear my throat, prepare myself to speak as Daphne, and the whole auditorium quiets down. But they're all turning their heads toward each other, as if to ask, "Where is Annabelle?"

"Thank you, Mr. Davis. I thought for days and days about what I would say in this moment, standing in front of all of you, the students, teachers, and community members of McManus Middle School. Every time I went to write the words down, I balled up the paper and tossed it in the recycling. The truth is, for me to really speak my mind, I had to do what I do best . . . make a vlog."

Someone screams, "Oh my goodness, sneak preview!"

"So without further ado, I present to you my latest and final vlog. I call this episode 'Daphne Tells the Truth.'"

Now everyone is looking confused.

John lowers the house lights and presses play. An image of me sitting in the paper supply closet fades in.

"I know you guys were probably expecting to see Daphne in her full fabulous gear, but I have a confession to make. The girl you've been watching on YouTube isn't real. She's a made-up persona, just created by a regular dorky girl who was trying to make friends. Allow me to introduce myself. My name is Annabelle Daphne Louis."

Everyone gasps.

"And I've been lying this whole time. I owe everyone a big apology, but especially my best friends here at McManus—John, Clairna, and Navdeep. I never meant for this social experiment to grow out of control. I didn't want to be famous. All I wanted were friends to turn to when my mom leaves with the Air Force to Afghanistan. But things got out of hand, and next thing I knew I was doing any and everything I could to cover it up. I didn't want any fame or fortune out of my YouTube channel, but I couldn't stop it from happening. So effective immediately, the *Daphne Doesn't* vlog is canceled. The money I've made from it will be donated to a good cause. I'm sorry if I hurt anyone, and I understand if no one ever wants to be my friend again."

The video fades to black. John raises the houselights, and there's a sea of frozen, shocked faces staring back at me.

I remove the wig and let my poofy, curly hair do what it does best—find its way toward the ceiling.

"So there you have it," I say into the microphone in my normal voice. "I am Annabelle Daphne Louis. Shy, sometimes funny, dorky, and proud of it. I don't do sports. I don't do drama. I don't do fashion. And if you saw my last vlog, I definitely don't dance."

The crowd cuts me off with laughter.

"But here is what I love doing: being with my friends, doing cool things with my video camera and computer, and spending time with my family, especially my mom . . . who I'm going to miss very, very much."

I'm fighting back the single tear that's building up in my left eye. And then the strangest thing happens. Clairna starts clapping. Then Nav, then Rachael shouts, "It's OK, Annabelle!" And one by one, the others join in.

I place my hands over my mouth to stop myself from crying yet again. Mom rushes to the stage to hug me, along with Mr. Fingerlin, who steps up to the microphone.

"The Louis family has a special presentation."

Mom speaks next. "Thank you, Pete. My daughter, Annabelle, is the kindest person I know. She did her research and found a wonderful organization to donate her earnings to. My husband and I contacted them and asked for a representative to be here tonight. Will Mr. Barry Ellis please come to the stage to receive a donation of three thousand dollars to the Military Kids United Camp?"

I see Rachael's face light up at the sound of that.

A tall man with a bald head and glasses walks up to receive the check. We take pictures for the newspaper, the *Linden Leader*. Every single person in the audience is clapping, and they keep clapping through Mr. Ellis's speech.

"I can't thank the Louis family enough for their generosity to donate money to our organization and for choosing to sponsor several well-deserving children to attend our camp next summer. Military Kids United serves children of members of our armed forces, but especially those children whose parents are deployed. Our organization provides a summer of fun for these children. We take them swimming, hiking, and on trips to experience new cultures and sights. We do all that we can to make sure that while our military is off protecting our freedom, their children are here in the United States, enjoying theirs. So once again, I say thank you, and I encourage Miss Annabelle to not give up on her YouTube channel. As you can see, the people love it. But I do have one suggestion. I know *Daphne Doesn't* is a funny way of talking about all the things you don't do. How about renaming it to *Annabelle Always* and posting videos about being true to the things you love. What do you think, audience?"

The crowd goes wild and starts screaming, "YES!"

I step forward and say, "That sounds like a good idea, sir."

John dims the houselights again. Mr. Davis screams in the microphone, "Let's continue the party, guys!"

The beat picks up, loud and proud. On my way down the stage stairs, people are patting me on the back, telling me I did a good job, and asking for selfies.

Outside of the big windows, the snow starts falling, letting everyone know that winter has made its entrance into Linden.

I feel a tap on my back. I turn around and see that it's Rachael. "I'm really—" I start.

"I think you've apologized enough for one day, Annabelle," she says. "That was really cool what you did—donating to the camp like that. And that's cool that you chose to sponsor some campers next summer. Those kids are really lucky."

"Yeah, I know. You're gonna love it!" A smile wraps around my whole face.

Rachael's eyes double in size. "Are you saying what I think you're saying?"

"I can't wait to hear all about it . . . that is, if you want to tell me. You don't have to. I understand that I messed up."

"Oh, shut up! You stop it right now!" Rachael grabs me hard and pulls me in for a hug.

"I heard your mom say that you wanted to go to that camp, but with everything your family was going through, it wasn't going to work out."

"Yeah, things have been hard between the divorce and the deployment. And I know I wasn't so nice to you. Can we start over?"

I hold out my hand to shake hers. "Friends?"

"Definitely."

Mom and Ms. Wright dance their way over to us.

Ms. Wright looks at Mom and mouths, "Thank you. For everything."

The song "True Friend" by Miley Cyrus comes on. John, Clairna, and Nav find their way to Rachael and me. No words are spoken. No further apologies are necessary.

We just start dancing to the beat, like old friends. Make that new ones. Because starting right here and right now, everything is brand-new again. This city. This school. These friends.

I dance my dorky heart out and whisper a wish to the sky. Six months will fly, but Mom will come back. And I've got the best "squad" around to help me get through it all.